Her heart twisted into a painful knot. If only she had a camera... Seeing him hold the little girl in a protective embrace, especially while he slept, couldn't have been more convincing evidence that he had more fathering instincts than he credited to himself.

Neither of them looked comfortable, so, taking a chance, Maggie lifted Breanna out of his embrace.

Joe hadn't budged an inch. Clearly he was exhausted.

Before she'd taken two steps, Joe shifted position, then suddenly bolted upright.

"Breanna?" he asked, his voice rusty.

"She's in her crib," she answered softly.

His tension visibly eased.

"Thanks." Then, apparently gaining more of his wits, he stared at her in surprise. "Maggie?"

"In the flesh," she said cheerfully. "I thought I'd check on you, and when you didn't answer the door I used your spare key. I hope you don't mind."

His suddenly wide smile transformed his face. "No, I don't. In fact, I'm glad you did. I was counting the hours until tomorrow morning when I'd see you again."

Words to warm a woman's heart...

Jessica Matthews's interest in medicine began at a young age, and she nourished it with medical stories and hospital-based television programmes. After a stint as a teenage candy-striper, she pursued a career as a clinical laboratory scientist. When not writing or on duty she fills her day with countless family and school-related activities. Jessica lives in the central United States with her husband, daughter and son.

Recent titles by the same author:

HIS BABY BOMBSHELL
THE ROYAL DOCTOR'S BRIDE
HIS LONG-AWAITED BRIDE

EMERGENCY: PARENTS NEEDED

BY
JESSICA MATTHEWS

MILLS & BOON®

First published in Great Britain 2009
Large Print edition 2010
Harlequin Mills & Boon Limited,
Eton House, 18-24 Paradise Road,
Richmond, Surrey TW9 1SR

© Jessica Matthews 2009

ISBN: 978 0 263 21101 6

Printed and bound in Great Britain
by CPI Antony Rowe, Chippenham, Wiltshire

To my readers.
Thanks for allowing me to
share my stories with you.

CHAPTER ONE

"THERE'S been a change in plans, Maggie."

Reporting for duty on Monday morning, Maggie Randall stopped in her tracks at Captain Keller's words. That particular phrase never heralded good news and she braced herself for the latest bombshell. Two weeks ago when the captain had said something similar, she'd gotten a new partner and her life hadn't been the same since.

Then again, maybe he had finally realized how partnering her with Joseph Donatelli had been a mistake, she thought hopefully. Perhaps he was about to announce that he would shuffle the duty roster and assign her to someone else, someone who understood the concept of compromise.

"Oh?" she asked.

"You'll work with Kevin Running Bear today," he said.

Kevin was a firefighter with emergency

medical technician training. Normally, he fought fires, but in a pinch he filled in on the ambulance crew. Apparently today was one of those move-people-around-to-cover-the-hole days, which meant that Joe must be playing hookey.

As crazy as it sounded, she was actually relieved. For the next twenty-four hours she could do her job in peace. No battles to fight. No justifying her every move. No opportunities for Joe to find fault with her decisions, complain about what he considered her overly friendly bedside manner or the length of time she spent with their patients.

And definitely there would be no chance of her knees turning weak when he flashed one of his lazy smiles at her. Being attracted to a man who could push her buttons without even trying was extremely irritating, which was probably why she practically bristled like a porcupine whenever they were together.

Needless to say, their little 'clashes', as she liked to call them, were making it extremely difficult to develop the rapport they needed to function together as a team. Doing so was important to her for no other reason than she'd never live with herself if a patient ultimately paid the price for their inability to get along.

"What happened to Joe?" she asked, half-surprised that he called in on such short notice. In the four years they'd both been employed by the Barton Hills Fire Department, Joe had received citations for his perfect attendance. Whatever had kept him from his shift must be serious indeed.

"He's taking a personal day," Captain Keller said.

A personal day? She may have only worked with Joe for the past two weeks since his temporary transfer to Station One, but the crews scattered among the three fire stations in Barton Hills were a close-knit group. Everyone knew everyone else and Joe's record for dependability was legendary. The man was the first to arrive—often an hour before his shift began—and the last to leave. Rumor had it that he'd work 24/7 if allowed to because he didn't have anyone waiting for him at home. Of course, that would cut into the steady stream of women he supposedly dated, but, regardless of his social life, he lived his job to the point that he only scheduled a vacation when he'd maxed out his earned time hours.

"Really?" she asked, incredulous.

He nodded. "Really. But before you break out the champagne…."

Her face warmed under her superior's chastening gaze. "I wouldn't," she protested weakly.

He raised an eyebrow, as if he knew she wasn't quite telling the truth. "Just remember, this is only for today."

She held back her sigh of disappointment. "I know."

He eyed her carefully. "Look, I'm aware that things aren't running like a well-tuned engine between you two, especially after the Hilda Myers incident."

Hilda was an elderly lady who suffered from anxiety attacks and called 911 on a regular basis. Maggie had befriended her and usually, after a short visit that was long enough to sample the cookies or cake that Hilda had so precipitously provided, the older woman was fine. Joe had taken exception to a call that he considered to be little more than a social visit and quietly began to dig into Hilda's history. The next thing Maggie knew, he'd gotten the captain, then the chief involved, and by the end of the week Hilda's family had moved her to an assisted living home. While Maggie had been working for weeks to convince Hilda to accept her limitations and relocate to a place of her choosing, she hated that the elderly lady hadn't been given the option to decide her own fate.

In truth, she didn't fault Joe for the final outcome—Hilda was finally in an environment that suited her needs, even if the older woman had been reluctant to take that step. However, what really rankled Maggie was how Joe had accomplished in a matter of days what she hadn't been able to accomplish in months. He was the full-steam-ahead sort while she was willing to look for a more circuitous solution.

"The problem is, you're both, shall we say, *strong willed,*" the captain continued, "but you each have partners on medical leave and pairing you two was the only logical decision Chief Watson could make."

This time she did sigh. "I suppose so."

He clapped her shoulder. "Cheer up. It's only until Bill and Robert get back on their feet. A few months, tops."

Her regular partner, Robert MacArthur, had missed a step at home and fallen down a flight of stairs, breaking an ankle. He'd undergone two surgeries and developed an infection after the second. Bill Reeves, Joe's partner at Station Two, had torn a rotator cuff in his shoulder, playing baseball with his teenage son. After surgery, he wasn't healing as fast as his doctor had hoped. As a result, both Joe and Maggie had been "orphaned" and rather than play musical partners, the chief had matched them on the paramedic duty roster.

In Maggie's opinion, it wasn't a match made in heaven.

"A few months," she echoed with a weak smile. She could handle anything for that length of time. Or so she hoped.

"You're both off for the next couple of days," Keller reminded her. "If I were you, I'd use the time to figure out a way to resolve your differences. Otherwise the next couple of months will stretch out mighty long for all of us. I don't want to referee your little skirmishes for the entire time."

Once again, the captain was right. Four months, less two weeks, could stretch out interminably, even with their twenty-four-hours-on, forty-eight-hours-off schedule.

"Yes, sir," she said, hoping he'd given Joe the same pep talk when he'd called in to take his personal day.

Maggie thought about the situation throughout her entire shift. Resolving their differences when they were rooted within completely different philosophies seemed an impossible task, but she had to do *something*.

The answer came in the late night hours as they often did when she was about to drift off to sleep. If Joe had called in to take an unscheduled personal day, he had to be sick. What man wouldn't appreciate someone giving him a little sympathy when he was suffering? Yes, she thought with some satisfaction, a bit of TLC was in order…

Joe saw the familiar older-model sedan with its front end folded like an accordion against a light pole. He jumped from his ambulance and ran forward, only to find Dee's head resting against the steering-wheel. Eyes closed, blood ran down her face from the cut on her forehead.

"Dee?" he urged, feeling a familiar panic as he recognized his victim was a friend. "Hang on and we'll get you out of there."

Her pale eyelids fluttered open. "Joe?"

He clasped her hand, noticing how cold her skin felt. "Yeah?"

"I'm glad you're here."

"Me, too." He turned to yell at the firefighters swarming over the vehicle. *"Hurry up. We need to get her out of there, now."*

"Joe?"

He met her gaze, determined to hide his worry in spite of the fear gripping his chest. *"Yeah?"*

"I can't feel my legs or my arms."

"Don't panic," he told her, trying to follow his own advice. *"We'll take care of you. I promise."*

"O...K." Dee's eyes closed, then burst open. *"The baby. Look after...the baby, Joe."*

Immediately Joe glanced into the backseat. Empty. No infant car seat, no baby paraphernalia. *"What baby, Dee?"* he asked. *"Whose baby?"*

"Mine," Deanna mumbled.

"Where is it?" he urged. *"I don't see a baby."*

"Take care...of...her." Dee gasped for air and began to act agitated. *"Promise."*

Trying to keep her calm and certain she was hallucinating, he said the only thing he could to a friend. *"I promise, but where is she?"*

Dee cocked her head. *"Can't you hear her, Joe?"*

He listened. *"I can't."*

"You have to, Joe. You're all she has."

This time, a distant wail of a baby caught his attention and he knew it was imperative that he *locate this child. But where should he look? "I hear her, Dee, but where is she?"*

"She's right here."

He glanced around the scene, afraid to find the broken body of a child thrown from the vehicle. Nothing. "I don't see her, Dee..."

Joe bolted upright in his easy chair, awakening to the now-familiar sinking feeling in the pit of his stomach before he realized he'd been dreaming again. He wasn't reliving a modified version of the accident that had taken the life of his old friend, Deanna Delacourt, and he wasn't frantically searching for a baby. He was at home, dozing in his easy chair, and Dee's daughter was sleeping in his spare bedroom, although at this particular moment she was wailing loud enough to wake the neighbors.

Muscles protesting as he unfolded his body to stand, he rubbed his gritty eyes before checking the time. 9:00 a.m. He'd gotten exactly three hours of uninterrupted sleep all night, which wasn't remarkable by itself. Working long stretches without a break wasn't uncommon when he was on duty because emergencies didn't occur on a schedule. He simply went home at the end of his shift, fell into his bed and caught up the hours he'd missed.

Unfortunately, his life wasn't as accommodating since little Breanna Delacourt had moved into his house. She was his to care for 24/7 whether he was exhausted or not, which meant his days of solitude had come to a swift end. Hell, at this rate, he'd have to go to work just so he could get some shut-eye.

Breanna's wails pierced his eardrums. "I'm coming, I'm coming," he said aloud to the empty room as he walked down the short hallway, rolling his shoulders to ease the ache and rubbing the last vestiges of sleep from his eyes.

"Good morning, little Bee," he told the eleven-month-old, who was sitting on her makeshift bed of blankets and a sleeping bag in the middle of the bedroom floor. "What's wrong?"

Breanna's mouth quivered as tears glistened on her eyelashes. From the way she eyed him, she'd obviously felt as if she were living her worst nightmare, too. And she probably was. Wanting her mother and getting him instead had to be as stressful for her as the situation was for him. He, at least, had the advantage of understanding what had happened but Breanna did not. She only knew that she wanted her old life with her mother, not this new one with a man she'd never met.

What were you thinking, Dee? he silently railed. *You knew I wasn't cut out to be the sort of father figure a kid needed.*

But whatever plane in the universe where Dee had gone didn't allow for two-way communication. He was on his own, left to devise a plan for a situation he hadn't anticipated in his wildest dreams. And at the moment the first thing to do was to sort out what Breanna wanted…

Uncomfortable in his new role as father, Joe had learned enough in his crash 'daddy' course to change her diaper and he did so with clumsy hands. He'd never felt as helpless as he did now— as he had for the past thirty-six hours. Nothing he did made the little girl happy and he'd already exhausted his small store of parenting ideas. He needed help…and fast. But who could he call?

Honestly, Dee, what made you think I was the best candidate to take care of your daughter?

His little voice corrected him. *Dee said you were all she had, remember?*

"She was wrong," he said aloud, ignoring the idea that denying Dee's claim didn't make it so.

The doorbell pealed and he frowned at the interruption. Dressing Breanna for the day would have to wait.

He freed her snuggle bunny from being buried in the blankets and tucked it next to her, hoping he could deal with his early morning guest before Breanna realized he'd left the room and raised the roof again.

A minute later, to Joe's amazement, he saw his fellow paramedic, Maggie Randall, fidgeting on his porch. She'd obviously come directly on her way home from the fire station because she still wore her blue uniform. Her long, tawny hair was restrained in her customary braid and her expression reflected the wariness he was coming to expect when she spoke to him.

He wasn't so physically and emotionally exhausted not to realize that he was responsible for the caution in her chocolate-brown eyes, but what could he expect? They'd butted heads from the very beginning and all because it was the only way he could counteract the electrical jolt a single, innocent and accidental touch had given his system. Right now, though, she was a familiar face and a welcome sight.

"Am I glad to see you," he said fervently.

She blinked, clearly taken aback by his declaration. "You are? Oh. Well, good morning to you, too." Her gaze swept over him, making him conscious of his babyfood-stained T-shirt, tousled hair and bare feet. "Sorry to show up unannounced, but you missed a shift so I thought I'd check on you and make sure everything was OK."

The concept of anyone questioning his absence and worrying about him was foreign and completely disconcerting, especially when Maggie was the one worrying. She was an attractive woman with a vivacious, caring personality that he found very appealing. For the hundredth time, he wished Maggie had chosen another field because she stirred him in ways he shouldn't be stirred if he wanted to keep their relationship on a professional footing.

"Actually, things aren't OK," he began.

Sympathy shone from her eyes. "I can see that. You look a little rough around the edges. The stomach bug going around right now is vicious." She thrust a container at him. "My mother swears there isn't anything that chicken-noodle soup can't cure, so I got up early and threw it together just for you."

The dish was still warm. Once again, it was humbling to realize Maggie had gone to the trouble when she didn't have to bother. It was even more humbling to think she'd made the effort when he hadn't exactly endeared himself to her. "How did you manage? You couldn't have had time to go shopping...."

"I didn't," she admitted. "I raided the cupboards at the station so I'll replace what I took the next time I'm on duty. It's no big deal."

Her effort may not be a big deal to her, but to him it was. "Thanks, but I'm—"

"Don't worry, I left out the arsenic."

Unable to help himself, he chuckled. "I wasn't worried. If anything happens to me, you'll be the first suspect."

Her smile lit up her face. "Exactly. However, if I were you," she continued as if she were in a hurry to leave now that she'd done her good deed, "I'd go back to bed and get some rest. Do you have the usual home remedies? Acetaminophen, decongestant, cough medicine, soda and crackers? If not, I'll be happy to run to the store or do whatever...."

"I'm not sick."

She hesitated. "You aren't?"

"Something came up," he began as an idea popped into his head and instantly took root. "Something personal."

"Oh." She took a step backward. From the way

her face turned a beautiful shade of pink as she eyed the bowl in his hand, she clearly regretted her kind action. "Then I'm sorry to bother you," she said stiffly.

"You aren't bothering me at all," he assured her. "In fact, you're the very person I need, Maggie."

Before she could do more than stare at him with a dumbfounded expression on her face, he grabbed her wrist and pulled her inside.

Maggie didn't know what threw her off center the most—the tingles his touch sent up her arm or the claim from the most independent, do-it-himself man she'd ever met that he needed *her.* Although her heart warmed at hearing the words, she also knew that being needed was her weak point. She hadn't fully recovered from the last time a man had taken advantage of her good nature with those words.

"Excuse me?" she asked politely as she found herself in his foyer, where she heard a baby wailing.

"I don't know who else to turn to," he admitted. "When you showed up on my doorstep… trust me when I say you're a gift from heaven."

She eyed him with suspicion, purposely staring

at his face to avoid the sight of his wide chest, the well-defined muscles under his snug-fitting gray T-shirt, and the runner's legs revealed by his athletic shorts. "A gift? Come on, Donatelli. This is me you're talking to, not one of your weekend bimbos. Are you sure you haven't been nipping the cough syrup?"

"I haven't taken a drop," he insisted. "I just need a few pointers…"

The wailing grew louder until she saw the source of the noise crawling toward them in a pink sleeper. The little girl with tousled light brown curls and a scowl on her pixie face dragged a lopeared bunny in a tight-fisted hand.

"You're babysitting?" she asked inanely.

A pained expression crossed his face. "No. Well, I am, but not in the true sense of the word. She's…." His voice faded and he rubbed his face.

"She's what, Joe?"

He hesitated. "She's…mine."

Joe? A father? It simply didn't compute. He'd never given any indication, never even *hinted* that he had a child, but he was a handsome man who didn't seem to lack female companionship. Nothing said he couldn't have an ex-wife in the picture, even if he hadn't shared that so-called picture with anyone.

His 'something personal' was definitely personal, but his new status struck her the most. She did *not* want to be attracted to another single father. Once had been enough.

"I thought you said you didn't have any family," she accused.

"I don't." He jerked a hand through his hair, leaving several strands askew. "Breanna is… It's a long story."

"I'm sure," she muttered under her breath. Certain she should steer clear of this situation because it was nothing more than an emotional minefield, she edged toward the door. "I should go and leave you two to…" She watched the baby maneuver herself into a sitting position at Joe's feet, where she continued to whimper. "To bond."

He reached out and held the door closed with one large hand. "Don't go. Please."

"You're busy, Joe, and I only stopped by to drop off the soup, which obviously wasn't necessary."

"I need you. Breanna needs you."

"Don't be silly," she said briskly, determined to stick to her non-involvement policy. "I just met her. What can I do?"

"Help me figure out why she won't stop crying. She's been like this since I got her."

Breanna stared up at Maggie with water-filled eyes and hiccuped her sobs. Maggie steeled herself against the tears, but when the little girl dropped to all fours and crawled forward until she grabbed Maggie's pant leg and pulled herself upright, Maggie knew she couldn't walk away.

She cast a disparaging glance at Joe before crouching down to the little girl's level. "Hi sweetie," she crooned. "What's wrong?"

Immediately, Breanna raised her arms and sniffled.

Maggie's heart hadn't hardened enough to deny this precious and clearly unhappy baby a hug. Giving in to the inevitable, she lifted the youngster off the floor and tucked her expertly on one hip as she swiped Breanna's tear-streaked face. "What's wrong with your world, little one?"

Breanna laid her head on Maggie's shoulder and quieted.

Joe mumbled something under his breath—something that sounded like 'what wasn't wrong?'

"What did you say?" she asked.

He rubbed his face at the same time his shoulders seemed to slump as if in relief. "Nothing." Then, "She likes you."

Maggie would have been perfectly satisfied if the little girl had ignored her and crawled in the opposite direction. "She just recognizes a soft touch."

"Soft touch or not, do you mind staying for a while? Until she settles down for longer than thirty seconds and my ears stop ringing?"

She wanted to refuse, but his hopeful expression, coupled with her own goal to begin building some sort of rapport with him, convinced her to agree. "OK, but only for a few minutes."

"Great. Have a seat while I fix her breakfast."

Maggie followed him into a small kitchen where the sink was overflowing with dirty dishes. From the way he paused to frown, then sigh at the sight, she suspected he was normally as meticulous in his house as he was on the job. Clearly, his daughter had upset his entire routine and style of living.

She sat at a table covered with pizza boxes and take-out containers as the little girl clung to her like a sandburr; nothing short of something drastic would convince her to let go, so Maggie simply let her hang on.

"To be honest, I expected to find you with your head in the toilet, not taking care of a baby," she commented, politely ignoring the mess.

"After the past two days, I wish you had," he said dourly.

Maggie chuckled, somewhat amused that she was finally seeing a different side to the organized, everything-in-its-place Joseph Donatelli. "It can't have been that bad."

"It was worse," he said glumly, rubbing the two days' worth of dark whiskers on his face before he began preparing baby formula with actions testifying to an obvious lack of experience. "I haven't slept for more than a few hours at a time and neither has she. I honestly don't know how she has the energy to keep going."

Strangely enough, his less-than-immaculate appearance only made him seem more human, more vulnerable, and far more appealing than he already was. He looked like a man in desperate need of a woman's touch and she had to stop herself from wanting to be the one to give it to him. As much as she hated to think that he'd denied his own child, she couldn't ignore the way he had to read directions for such a simple task. OK, so he didn't talk about his daughter, but maybe he had a good excuse… Maybe her mother lived in another state; maybe he didn't have access to his child until now, maybe it was too painful to discuss a baby who wasn't a part of his life. But whatever the reason, as her partner, he deserved the benefit of the doubt.

"You haven't done this very often, have you?" she asked softly, noticing how he spilled the formula as he poured it into a bottle and struggled to attach the nipple.

"Clearly, my incompetence shows," he said wryly.

"I wouldn't call it incompetence," she said, trying to minimize his obvious failing. "Awkwardness, perhaps, but if you do anything often enough, it will become second nature. Before long, you'll be able to fix her formula in your sleep."

He cast a baleful glance in her direction. "Mixing formula is one thing. Understanding what to do to keep her from crying all day long is another."

"Given enough time, you'll learn that, too," she predicted. "Didn't you spend any time with her while her mom was around so she'd learn you weren't a stranger?"

"No."

"Then maybe you should call her and explain the problems you're having," she suggested. "She may—"

"No." He shook his head for emphasis. "I can't."

How typical of the Joe Donatelli she knew. He could never admit failure, never admit he might be wrong or couldn't handle a situation. She wanted to think his Italian heritage came into play, but she had enough males in her family to suspect his stubbornness was just a guy thing.

"Of course you can," she said impatiently. "Admitting you're out of your depth isn't the end of the world."

"Her mother's dead," he said flatly. "I'm on my own."

Dead? He had a far bigger problem than she'd realized... "I'm sorry," she murmured.

He raked his hair with one hand. "That makes two of us."

"I assume it was recent," she said slowly, testing his reaction.

Silently, he brought a small bowl of baby cereal and a jar of strained peaches to the table, then mixed some of the formula into the cereal. His jaw was clenched, and Maggie waited for his answer.

Finally, he nodded. "A week ago. Car accident on the other side of town. She apparently hydroplaned and struck a telephone pole."

Maggie thought for a moment. "Oh, yes. I remember reading about the accident in the newspaper. That was Breanna's mother?"

"Yeah," he admitted gruffly. "That was Dee."

"If I remember right, the guys from Station Two responded."

"We did."

Suddenly, it all became clear. He'd been more taciturn than usual on that particular Friday when they'd worked together. She'd assumed his grumpiness had been because he'd pulled an extra shift at Station Two on his regular day off to cover their staff shortage, but obviously she'd been wrong.

"And you were on the scene," she guessed.

Again he nodded, his eyes bleak. "Yes."

Maggie leaned back in her chair and stared at him as he began feeding Breanna, hardly able to reconcile everything she'd learned with her own perceptions. It was always difficult to lose a victim, but to *know* that individual on a personal level made it even more so. "I'm so sorry," she said again. "You should have told us."

"It wouldn't have changed the final outcome."

"No, but we could have supported you in your loss." Then she added, "Do the guys at Station Two know?"

"I told them Dee and I were friends. Which we were."

"Friends who had a baby." Her mind raced with scenarios and possibilities of why Joe hadn't told anyone about his daughter. Either he didn't trust anyone with the information or he was as shallow in his relationships as Arthur had been. Neither option sat well.

"I know what you're thinking, but you'd be wrong." His voice was hard.

She raised an eyebrow. "Just what am I thinking, Donatelli?"

"That I walked out on her, leaving her to face her pregnancy alone, but I didn't. I *wouldn't*."

Pain appeared in his dark eyes for an instant before it disappeared. "The last time I saw Dee, she didn't have a steady boyfriend and she certainly didn't look or say she was expecting. Naturally, when she talked about her daughter while we were working on her..." He paused, then cleared his throat before he continued, "I thought she was confused and imagining things because she'd always wanted a houseful of kids."

Dee may not have been confused, but Maggie definitely was. Breanna was Joe's daughter, yet when he'd known her mother, Dee hadn't been seeing anyone and she supposedly hadn't been pregnant.

"I didn't know Breanna existed," he went on, "until Dee's attorney contacted me the other day. I was apparently named in her will as Breanna's guardian if anything happened to her."

Now the scenario made sense. Joe wasn't the deadbeat dad she'd feared, denying the existence of his own child. He was a man who'd been granted custody of a friend's baby. "I assume her father isn't in the picture?"

He visibly winced and for a long moment didn't answer. When he finally spoke, he sounded weary. "According to Breanna's birth certificate, you're looking at him."

CHAPTER TWO

HE WAS a father. The concept was so completely foreign to him that Joe couldn't make sense of it no matter how many times he repeated the fact. A father. A dad. A *parent.* Fate was surely having a laugh at his expense.

What the hell were you thinking, Dee? he silently railed for what seemed the hundredth time. *You knew fatherhood wasn't in my plans.*

He wanted to wash away the past few days as easily as he washed away the smoke clinging to his body after a fire, but life didn't work that way. He had to deal with the aftermath as best as he could, and right now that meant doing whatever was necessary to keep Breanna calm when he'd rather howl with her.

The only bright spot was that at this moment he wasn't alone. Maggie was here, being an anchor at a time when he desperately needed one. Although, at the moment, his so-called anchor looked as if someone had pulled the rug out from under her.

"You're her father? Her real, *biological* father?"

If the situation wasn't so dire, he would have found humor in Maggie's surprise. "So the paperwork says."

"The paperwork," she repeated. "You mean, you don't know for certain?"

"No, I don't. Dee and I… Our physical relationship was…" he winced as he chose his words carefully in the interest of full disclosure "…very short-lived. It didn't take long for us to realize we were better friends than lovers, which was what we were during the entire time I knew her," he insisted.

She raised an eyebrow. "I see. How old is Breanna?"

"Eleven months."

"When did you meet Dee?"

He thought for a minute. "Not quite two years ago."

Maggie's brow furrowed as if she were doing the math. "The timeframe fits." From the doubt on her features, she didn't believe his relationship with Dee had been based on friendship, not sex. Considering the child on her lap, if he wore her shoes, he wouldn't either.

Circumstantial evidence, in his opinion. "I know this situation doesn't show me in a favorable light, but Dee and I were only friends," he insisted. "And she wasn't the sort of woman to sleep around."

"I'm not anyone's judge and jury, Joe. You don't owe me any explanations," she said.

For reasons he didn't understand, Maggie's opinion mattered. Perhaps it was the way she looked at him. Perhaps it was because he was still trying to find his footing with her as his new partner and feeling as if he was failing miserably. Perhaps it was because he wanted to see respect in her eyes when she looked at him. Perhaps he was afraid that if he wasn't completely honest and utterly transparent, she'd leave him to face this alone. Right now, that was too frightening a fate to consider.

"But the fact remains—and I'm not doubting you—Breanna *could* be yours."

He shook his head. "We had sex once—*once*—and it was very early in our relationship."

She raised an eyebrow. "You know the drill. It only takes a single swimmer to create a baby."

"We were careful," he insisted, not willing to believe their precautions had failed.

"If you say so," she said agreeably, as if she were only humoring him. "And if that's true—and I'm not saying it isn't—then you believe Dee's trying to foist someone else's baby on you?"

"Yes. No." He ran a hand through his hair. As close as they had become, it seemed out of character for Dee to have been secretly dating someone on a regular basis. If she hadn't had a steady romantic interest, Breanna could have been the result of a one-night stand, in which case Dee might have been too embarrassed to admit it.

More importantly, though, after all the hours they'd spent talking about their shared histories, it seemed odd that she'd pass another man's baby off on him when she'd known his decision about parenthood was unchangeable. "I don't know. She never mentioned she was keeping company with anyone else, but that doesn't mean she wasn't."

And yet, realizing that she'd hidden her pregnancy from him after they'd been so open with each other was a huge disappointment.

"Then I hate to tell you this, Donatelli, whether you want to believe it or not, you're the logical suspect."

Admittedly, he was, but there still had to be some mistake. Birth control was something he believed in wholeheartedly and he never took shortcuts or relied on the woman to assume responsibility. Because he didn't think he could be too careful, he always controlled that aspect of his life. No exceptions. *Ever.*

"I asked the lawyer for a paternity test."

"And?"

"He'll make the arrangements and will let me know where to be and when."

Her expression was inscrutable. "What happens in the meantime? DNA testing could take a few weeks."

According to the lawyer, Joe was looking at a two-to-three-week wait, give or take, and that wasn't counting the time to schedule an appointment. As this situation didn't warrant immediate, overnight service, Dee's attorney wasn't in favor of rushing the process, so Joe guessed it would take three to four weeks from start to finish.

Four weeks to assume the monumental task of looking after Dee's daughter. Four weeks to know the truth. Four weeks that seemed like an eternity.

"I'll do the best I can," he said honestly.

"And if you're not her father?" She raised an eyebrow. "What then, Donatelli?"

Funny how he was learning that when she called him by his last name, she was exasperated with him. Hell, right now he was exasperated with himself and everyone else, especially with Dee for dumping him in this no-win situation.

"I should give her to someone who *wants* to be a parent," he said, testing her reaction. "Someone who's more capable and better suited to raise a child."

"Who says you aren't capable?"

"I do," he said tersely.

"I see," she said, although her expression held more curiosity and speculation than certainty. "Then why wait? Why not relinquish your legal responsibility now?"

Why not, indeed? The fact was, two very compelling reasons had prompted his wait-and-see decision. If Breanna was truly his, he'd be damned if he'd follow in his father's footsteps and abandon her. Of course, that raised the question of what he'd do if she wasn't his daughter. The answer would be easy, if not for one minor, yet mighty detail.

He exhaled slowly. "I made a promise."

"I see." She looked thoughtful. "How does the saying go? 'Promises are made to be broken'?"

"Not mine," he said firmly. He'd learned through bitter experience that a man's word was the most valuable thing he owned. He couldn't ignore that truth simply because it was convenient.

On the other hand, were verbal agreements valid when they were elicited without full disclosure? At the time, he would have sworn anything to keep Dee calm. Would he have been as quick to tell her what she'd wanted to hear if he'd known of Breanna's existence, if he'd really known what he was pledging to do?

He'd obviously said the right words because a wide, approving smile stretched across Maggie's face. "You're a good man, Donatelli," she said gruffly, "even if you don't think you're the best man for the job."

"How can I be?" he asked. "I'm a single guy."

"Lots of single parents, including men, raise kids."

"I don't have any idea how to take care of a baby, much less a little girl."

"You'll learn."

He began to pace. "You don't understand. I'm

the last person a kid needs as a father figure. My own—" He cut himself off.

"Yes…?" she coaxed. "Your own…what?"

He didn't want to explain and never felt the need to share the sordid tale. Dee was the only person who'd ever heard his story, but that had only been because she'd been a kindred spirit— a young woman who'd shared his experience. For his entire life, he'd placed that history into a small box he'd labeled "Keep Out" and stored it in the back of his memory while he'd gone to school and made a successful, rewarding career for himself. He'd built his life the way he wanted it and he was happy being a carefree, no-strings-attached bachelor.

At the same time, he knew Maggie would never understand his position if he didn't explain. As soon as he did, she'd agree he wasn't the best man for the job.

"My home life was dysfunctional, to say the least," he said, omitting specifics. "My mother died when I was a baby and when I was five, my father disappeared, leaving me in foster care. By the time I was ten, I'd decided that parenting wasn't in my future. I'm thirty years old and don't have the first clue about dealing with a kid, much less a baby."

To his surprise, Maggie didn't gasp in horror, although he saw the sympathy in her eyes. "I'm sorry you didn't grow up under ideal conditions," she said softly, "but I know who you are today, Joe. I've seen you interact with children when we've worked accidents. You aren't as incompetent as you think."

"Handling a youngster during an emergency situation is different than in a day-to-day situation," he added impatiently. "I don't know the first thing about finding a sitter or a doctor. Then there's formula and baby food, clothing sizes, and God only knows what else! What I know about a child's daily needs would fit in a teaspoon."

She shrugged. "Then you'll learn. Do you think first time parents learn those things by osmosis, that it's magically downloaded into their brains during delivery?"

OK, so maybe he could cope with the physical stuff like diapers and formula and clothing sizes, but the emotional aspect scared him spitless. How could he possibly give the love and support Breanna needed when he had nothing in his own experience to use as a pattern?

"I can't screw up her life," he said flatly.

"Giving up already?"

Her expression was inscrutable, but Joe sensed her disapproval. And if she disapproved of him breaking his promise, he could imagine the response he'd get from his superiors—quintessential family men—as well as the guys who worked alongside him in the trenches. None of them would understand; they'd only see the situation as one where he didn't live up to the duties that a dead woman had given him, regardless of who had fathered her child. That was a big deal to men who safeguarded people and property at all costs.

He rubbed his eyes. "Promise or not, she'd be better off with a stable couple who wants children."

"Dee apparently wanted you to do the honors," she reminded him.

Dammit, Dee! Why did you drag me into this? And if Breanna is mine, why didn't you tell me? Prepare me?

But she hadn't and now he had to deal with this mess as best as he could. If the situation simply didn't work out, then his conscience would be appeased, but he owed it to Dee to try his best in the meantime.

Which meant he needed a crash course on parenting from someone with experience…

Half resigned and half scared out of his wits at his fate, he met her gaze. "Regardless of what Dee was thinking, I can't take on Breanna alone."

"Once the guys at the station hear what happened, their wives will offer more help than you can ever imagine."

He shook his head as his answer stood before him. "Not good enough. Oh, I'm sure they'll be happy to pitch in once in a while or when I'm on duty, but what about the rest of the time?"

"You'll function like every other single father. You'll look after her, take her wherever you go, play with her, and pray for nap time."

"And what if I have a problem, like today? I need someone I can depend on, day or night." He turned a steady gaze on her. "Someone like my *partner.*"

Her jaw dropped. "Me? Why me?"

"Because you're perfect. You're single, so I wouldn't feel guilty calling you at all hours, and you're a woman so you're a natural at the nurturing stuff." As she sputtered, he continued, "You're also the one with the huge family, scads of nieces and nephews. You have an instinct with kids. Why, look at the miracle you performed in the last thirty minutes."

"Yes, but—"

"I need someone to teach me what to do. With your family experience, you're the best candidate. The *only* candidate."

No, Maggie screamed inside. As sorry as she was about his tough childhood, he should rely on someone who wanted the job. Joe's suggestion was out of the question. Simply. Out. Of. The. Question.

"No," she said, shaking her head for emphasis. "I'm not your man, or your woman as the case may be."

He seemed surprised by her answer. "Why not? You love children."

"I have my reasons."

"Oh?"

His raised eyebrow made it plain that he was waiting for an explanation. He would wait for a long time, she thought wryly. For one thing it was too painful to discuss and for another she didn't care to admit she'd been duped by a man who'd played her as expertly as a cellist played his instrument.

"I won't discuss them," she said stiffly. "Rest assured, my reasons are valid."

"And mine aren't?"

"OK," she conceded, "maybe we both have good excuses but—"

"I'd heard via the grapevine that you'd almost married a guy with two kids."

"'Almost' is the operative word," she quipped to hide the ache that hadn't completely disappeared. "Your situation is different."

"Because we aren't sleeping together?" he asked. "If that's what it takes…"

A tingle shot through her—a completely unwarranted tingle that started low in her belly and moved upward as a mental picture instantly developed in living color in her mind's eye. A second later, she wiped away the image and shifted her weight to stop the electricity skittering across her nerve endings.

"Don't be crude," she snapped, as irritated by her response as by his offer. "I loved him and I loved…" her throat suddenly closed "…those little boys. Your circumstances don't compare."

"Dee's daughter needs you as much as those two did, if not more. They had their father. She has no one except me and I'm not doing such a hot job."

As if he needed to remind her of the little girl's need while the infant sat on her lap and clutched Maggie's shirt with one tiny fist. He had to state the obvious, which was guaranteed to tug at her heartstrings. "You're not playing fair."

"No, I'm not. If you expect me to have a *hope* of raising Breanna properly, I need your help."

An image of Zach and Tyler flashed into her head. She hadn't seen them for more than a year. Their father had decided to move back to Montana so he could leave his memories of his dead wife behind and renew his relationship with his high-school sweetheart. As soon as she'd re-covered from the shock that he hadn't recipro-cated her love in spite of what she considered evidence to the contrary, she'd realized she'd simply been his stopgap measure. He'd used her to buy himself time to get over the proverbial hump of losing his wife and learning to deal with his two children. Once he had, he'd moved on.

And now Joe was asking her to put herself in the same position of being used again. Well, she couldn't do it. She *wouldn't*. She'd sworn off getting emotionally entangled with a man who had children and she wasn't going to reverse her decision even if he had become a parent overnight.

"You don't know what you're asking," she said flatly, trying to ignore Breanna's sweet baby scent or the way she leaned against her with complete trust. "As you know, my story didn't end on a happy note."

"His loss."

If the truth were known, it was more hers than his because she'd invested her heart and soul into their relationship, but she wouldn't dwell on that right now. "I won't let myself get emotionally involved again."

"Says the woman who does it more often than not. Dare I mention the Hilda Myers situation?"

"According to what you so kindly pointed out at the time, you consider my emotional involvement to be a character flaw," she countered.

He shrugged. "At times. At others, like now, it's a strength."

"In this case, it *is* a flaw," she insisted. "I already know what will happen. I'll grow attached to Breanna and then one day it'll all be over!" *I'm twenty-eight and once again I'll be left with nothing.*

"I can argue the same," he said. "You could meet some guy and next thing I know, you and Mr. Maggie are having juniors and juniorettes all over the place."

Oddly enough, his description startled her out

of her panic and she laughed. "Mr. Maggie? Junior and juniorette?"

"You know what I mean." He sounded impatient.

What he didn't understand was that being with him day in and out was as dangerous to her peace of mind as becoming Breanna's temporary mother figure. If she struggled with her attraction to Joe when they were on duty, how much more difficult would it be to keep her heart intact if she spent her free time with him as well?

"The point is," he continued, "I won't consider keeping Breanna unless I have someone I can depend on. Someone who has my back, so to speak."

"You can't dump your decision on *my* shoulders, Donatelli."

He raised an eyebrow, his eyes cool. "After Hilda's case came to a head, you accused me of not supporting you. 'We didn't function as a team,' you said. This is our chance to do that, Maggie, or were you just paying lip service to the concept? Does your philosophy of teamwork only apply when it suits you?"

"I was talking about supporting each other *on the job,*" she stressed. "I wasn't referring to our personal lives. They're separate."

"Only to a degree," he pointed out. "Can you honestly say you wouldn't have a problem working with me if I turned Breanna over to Social Services? That you wouldn't treat me differently because I didn't measure up to your standards?"

She bit her lip. Knowing he'd avoided his responsibilities probably would affect her opinion of him. And if she lost her respect for him because she questioned his decision-making ability, how could she ever hope they would function efficiently in an emergency?

"What about all these women you date?" she asked, desperate to provide another solution. "Surely one of them would be happy to—"

"*You're* the one I want—the one I trust," he said firmly.

"I'm flattered, but—"

"You're asking me to face my fears," he pressed on. "Yet you're not willing to face yours. You want me to commit to a job that will last for the next twenty years and beyond, but you aren't willing to invest a few months or a year of your time? Talk about a double standard."

She fell silent as the little girl rested against her chest as if she'd settled in Maggie's lap for the duration. In fact, if she didn't know better, she'd suspect this baby was doing her part to convince her to take on this new role.

"Would you really give up Breanna in spite of your promise to Dee if I don't help you?" she asked.

"In a heartbeat," he stated with clear conviction. "I know my limitations and I can't do this by myself. Better for her to go to a loving couple now rather than later."

The little girl fit in Maggie's arms as if she belonged there. Holding her was bittersweet. "This is blackmail."

"It's common sense," he corrected. "And I'm desperate, Maggie. If you don't agree…"

His pleading expression and helpless shrug tugged on her sympathies. As competent as he was as a paramedic, caring for a baby was clearly out of his comfort zone.

"How about this? If you'll hold my hand until the paternity test results are released, we'll re-evaluate the situation then."

"In other words, you're giving us both a way out."

"We'll re-evaluate," he repeated. "We both want what's best for Breanna, whatever that might be."

While that was true, his lack of commitment concerned her. Because of it, could she handle helping him with the baby in the meantime? She frowned, remembering her experiences with Tyler and Zach—how she'd helped with their bedtime rituals, fixed their breakfasts, received the handpicked bouquet of dandelions when they'd played outside.

Even after all this time, the loss hurt.

As she glanced at Joe, the hope in his eyes tipped the scales in his favor. He *was* her partner and he needed her. She'd also promised her chief to do what she could to mend their differences. If word got around that she refused to help Joe when it was in her power to do so, she'd suffer the consequences.

She didn't have a choice, she thought with resignation. Because she didn't, she would treat this situation with the same emotional detachment she used in her job. Her weakness for babies would be a drawback, but this time she wasn't expecting a happily-ever-after. Her eyes were wide open and no matter how events transpired, she wouldn't allow herself to forget that she was simply a stopgap measure, a temporary solution.

As long as she remembered that, it would be easy to guard her heart.

"OK," she said reluctantly. "I'll help until you have your answers from the lab. Then you'll have to sink or swim on your own."

"Fair enough."

But later, as they rearranged Joe's spare bedroom to accommodate the baby furniture he had yet to retrieve from Dee's apartment, she wondered if she hadn't made a deal with the devil.

It was absolutely amazing to see the difference Maggie's presence had made in just a few hours. Breanna had stopped her constant crying and had even giggled a few times when Maggie had played peek-a-boo. Joe had been able to take a long, relaxing shower instead of barely giving himself time to get wet, because Maggie had kept the little girl occupied. By the time he'd finished, Maggie had also washed his dishes and tidied the main living areas so his home looked neat and clean, rather than the disaster area it had become.

If he'd thought she wouldn't take offense and run off in a huff, he would have kissed her.

"How did you do it?" he asked as he surveyed the rooms.

She looked puzzled. "How did I do what?"

"Do your chores and keep Breanna happy at the same time?"

She laughed at his amazement. "It wasn't hard—you just go about your business. Don't worry, you'll get the hang of it."

"Somehow I doubt it."

"You will," she promised.

"So what did you do to Breanna to keep her happy?"

"Nothing," she said.

"Nothing?"

"Not a thing," she said. "I suspect she was simply reacting to your negative energy. Your nervousness and anxiety made her nervous and anxious and the only way she could express her emotions was by crying. As you can see, she's fine."

And she was. Breanna sat on the floor, cheerfully banging a wooden spoon on a plastic bowl and babbling.

"Wow. I'm amazed. Awed. And thoroughly intimidated."

Her laugh did funny things to his chest and he wanted to hear the sound again and again. "In a few days," she assured him, "you'll be an old pro."

He was skeptical. "If you say so."

"Anyway, I took the liberty of going through Breanna's things and made a list of what she'll need. You might want to pick up these things today, unless you have a stash of disposable diapers and formula that I didn't find."

"No stash." Joe took the list Maggie had made and read the items recorded in her handwriting. Man, he was in trouble if he thought her handwriting was sexy! Maybe it was time he started living up to his reputation, but surprisingly enough the handful—not hordes—of women he'd spent time with recently faded into insignificance when he compared them to Maggie.

"In that case, I've done all I can. I'll just get out of your hair…"

The thought of her leaving him to handle the baby on his own was scarier than a rescue on a construction scaffold. He caught her arm, conscious of her soft skin. "No, wait."

She paused. "Did you need something else?"

Hell, yes, he needed something else! He needed Maggie to stay with him, to be his safety net. Knowing that he wasn't Breanna's sole caretaker had done wonders for his peace of mind. The sensation of drowning because he was in over his head had eased and he wasn't eager for that suffocating feeling to return. It would, just as soon as she walked out the door.

"I'd hoped you could spend the day with us," he admitted. "Between your list and my plan to pick up Breanna's furniture at her mother's apartment, an extra pair of hands would be nice." He flashed her his most pleading expression, hoping she couldn't resist.

"I haven't gone home since I left work," she pointed out. "I'm still wearing my blues, for pete's sake. I'd really like to change into something else."

He ran his gaze over her, noticing as he had on days past how well she filled out the unisex department-issue clothing. The good thing about the blue uniform was that it only hinted at what it hid while street clothing usually did not. As she'd mentioned it, though, he wouldn't mind seeing her in an outfit that she had chosen. Jeans, a skirt, a form-fitting T-shirt that clung to her curves all came to mind... Suddenly, giving her time to change clothes seemed like a wonderful idea.

"Not a problem. We'll follow you home and then leave from your place." He sounded over-eager, even to his own ears. "Unless you have plans? Then we can come over later."

"No specific plans," she said slowly. "At least, nothing that can't wait a few hours."

Relief filled him as he grabbed her hand with both of his and squeezed. "Thanks, Maggie. I really appreciate it."

"You're…you're welcome."

She sounded breathless, as if she wasn't quite sure of what to make of his impulsive yet enthusiastic gesture.

He wasn't certain either, but the sensation of her palm against his and the strength in her fingers that belied the fine bone structure coalesced into a desire to pull her into his arms and hold her tightly against him.

However, patience and restraint were lessons he'd learned and things he practiced since he'd been a child. To ignore those lessons was asking for trouble, but he was also a strong believer in taking an opportunity as it presented itself.

Reluctantly, he released her hand. "Shall we go?"

Ten minutes later, he and Breanna walked into Maggie's house and he was instantly struck by how perfectly suited Maggie was for the task facing him. Her home was cozy and welcoming, with its framed pencil sketches and watercolors on the walls, the large throw pillows and fuzzy afghans hanging from an oak quilt rack. The house was neat and tidy, but it was obvious that everything inside had been selected for comfort rather than style. It was a house in which a person could kick back and relax, a house with a peaceful, contented atmosphere.

In less time than he expected, Maggie returned from her bedroom to rejoin him in the living room. She looked different, almost unrecognizable, and his inner peace shifted to purely masculine interest.

Her uniform had always told him that she was just "one of the guys". However, as she stood before him in street clothes, he saw her in an entirely new light.

Her faded and soft-from-numerous-washings denim jeans hugged her slim hips and long legs. The lime green V-neck T-shirt clung to her torso and revealed a modest amount of cleavage. A pair of sandals showed off red-painted nails and a silver ring on her second toe.

To think all this had been hiding under the regulation light blue shirt and utilitarian navy blue pants! Oh, the unisex cut of the clothing hadn't completely disguised what lay underneath; her feminine shape had filled the fabric in ways that the rest of the crew couldn't, but he'd had no idea just how mouth-watering her form really was.

Or maybe it was simply a case of knowing she was beyond his reach, so he'd never let himself imagine…but now, uniform or not, he'd never look at her the same way again.

CHAPTER THREE

THEY passed the drive to Dee's house in silence. Maggie knew Joe wasn't the talkative sort, so she didn't find his lack of conversation unusual. He maintained his usual calm, stoic expression as if he didn't consider this more important than any other errand, but as she studied him unobtrusively—he couldn't be *that* unmoved by their tasks or the reason behind them, could he?—she soon found several chinks in his armor.

His mouth had a pinched quality and his eyes, when he accidentally met her gaze, appeared positively haunted. His shoulders seemed permanently squared, as if he needed a military posture to maintain his composure. Strangely enough, knowing that he wasn't as unaffected as he appeared only made her more sympathetic toward him.

Fortunately, Dee's neighbor and Breanna's old

babysitter, Hannah Lightner, was at home, so she looked after the toddler while Maggie and Joe let themselves into Dee's apartment.

The place was eerily quiet, as if it were mourning its missing occupant. *Stop being fanciful,* she scolded herself. *It's only four walls.*

But, walls or not, the spirit of Dee seemed to hover overhead, especially when Maggie entered the bedroom and saw a pile of green silk—a nightgown—lying on the bed. Joe must have sensed it too because for the first time since they'd arrived, he looked uneasy. Then again, perhaps coming here only emphasized the new set of responsibilities that had landed on his shoulders without warning or preparation.

Feeling as if she was intruding on his private moment, Maggie headed to the baby's bedroom. Joe followed on her heels, as if he didn't want to be left alone with his memories.

"What should we load first?" she asked, determined to be as upbeat as possible in the face of his somber mood.

"The crib, I'd guess. I'll get my toolbox from the truck while you pack Breanna's clothes."

Within an hour, everything from the crib to the changing table to a stroller and clothing were stacked in the back of Joe's truck. "We'll pack up Dee's things later," he said as they secured the furniture for travel. "We have a few weeks before the rent is due, so that'll give us time to figure out what to do with her stuff."

"That didn't take long," Hannah declared as they reappeared on her doorstep.

"We only took the baby's things," Joe told her. "We'll take care of the rest another day. How's she been?"

"Oh, fine," Hannah said. "She's always been such a good baby. I've never had any trouble with her at all."

Joe nodded, but his mouth was pressed into a hard line. Obviously Hannah's well-meant remarks only emphasized Joe's feelings of inadequacy. Maggie would have to find ways to build his confidence and increase his comfort level with the little girl, although doing so in the space of a few hours seemed a monumental task.

"I'm just glad I was home today and could help," Hannah continued, blithely unaware of Joe's set jaw. "I'm going to miss her. I'll miss them both."

Sensing Joe's tension, Maggie stepped in. "As will a lot of people," she said. "But we thank you for your time and now we'll get out of your way so you can enjoy the rest of your day off."

"Of course." Hannah led them inside.

Maggie was prepared to see Breanna sitting on the floor, playing with a stack of plastic building blocks, but she hadn't prepared herself for what came next.

"Mama?" the little girl asked Maggie.

Oh, dear. The one word, uttered with just the right amount of hope and uncertainty, nearly undid her. She wanted nothing more than to escape, to leave this temporary child-rearing task to someone else, but she wasn't a quitter, or so she told herself before turning a smile on the little girl.

"Hi, sweetheart," she said. "Daddy's here."

Breanna went to Hannah, the one familiar constant in her life. "Mama?" she asked.

Hannah's eyes became suspiciously moist. "No, sweetie. Mama's not here. But your daddy is."

Maggie glanced at Joe. The man who'd always seemed as steady as a rock and completely fearless now appeared as if he were living his worst nightmare.

In his mind, he probably was.

"It's time to go, Breanna," he said, his voice unnaturally gruff.

Breanna studied him with eyes far too serious for a child her age. "Mama?"

Hannah shrugged apologetically. "She must be waiting for Dee to take her home."

The notion sent a flash of pain through Maggie's chest. Right now, Breanna wouldn't understand why she suddenly had a hole in her young life—she would only know that she did. It would fall on Joe to make sure this child never felt abandoned because of her loss.

Joe turned to Maggie. His eyes reflected indecision. "Now what? I'd rather not drag her out of here, kicking and screaming."

"Let's see what she does in a few minutes," Maggie suggested. She turned to Hannah. "Do you mind?"

"Not at all. If you like, I'll tell you what I know about her schedule."

So, for the next half-hour, Maggie listened and took mental notes, hoping Joe was absorbing a fraction of the information he was hearing. From the vacant expression on his face, she suspected he was still overwhelmed by the situation. She would need to fill the gap until he found his footing.

Before long, Breanna crawled onto the sofa and sat between them as she eyed Joe cautiously.

"She hasn't been around many men," Hannah remarked. "You're a novelty."

Maggie found that innocently volunteered tidbit interesting. In her opinion, it added evidence to the case that Joe—not another man—was Breanna's father. "Then Deanna wasn't seeing anyone?"

Hannah shook her head. "If she was, she kept him a secret, which wouldn't have been easy with us living next to each other. Although there was a fellow…" She looked thoughtful.

"And?" Joe raised an eyebrow.

"I saw him with her once or twice a long time ago, but she never introduced us. Then he quit coming and Dee never mentioned his name. Ever."

Maggie exchanged glances with Joe. "Would you recognize him if you saw him again?"

"Possibly. Like I said, it was a long time ago. He reminded me of you," she addressed Joe, "but not as tall. A little older. He dressed really well, too." Her face flushed. "Not that you looked like a bum, but this guy always wore a suit."

"Could he be Breanna's father?" Joe asked.

Hannah shook her head. "I doubt it."

"Why do you say that?" Joe asked.

"Because Dee said you were a tough act to follow," Hannah said bluntly.

A tough act to follow? Maggie was surprised to hear Joe described in such glowing terms. Clearly Dee's Joe Donatelli was a different man than her Joe Donatelli, she thought with some exasperation.

Feeling guilty for her uncharitable thought, she mentally backpedaled. OK, so he may not be an outgoing, blurt-out-everything-he-was-feeling sort, but her colleagues said he was a kind, honest, dependable person. Just because she hadn't personally seen indisputable evidence of those traits didn't mean it wasn't so.

For an instant, she was almost jealous of a dead woman. Clearly Dee hadn't had any trouble penetrating his outer shell, especially if his friendship with her had lasted longer than their physical relationship. Maggie should be able to accomplish the same.

The more she thought, the more she realized that in spite of her reluctance to help him with Breanna she wanted to meet the same Joe Donatelli who Dee Delacourt had obviously loved.

At seven o'clock that evening, Joe gratefully sank into the rocking chair as he fed Breanna her bedtime bottle of formula. The little girl had been fed her nighttime snack, bathed, and was now resting in his lap as she clutched her bunny. Joe hoped she'd exhausted herself to the point where she'd sleep all night because he certainly would if he got the chance.

His day hadn't been tiring in a physical sense, but he'd definitely been through an emotional wringer. It had been tough to visit Dee's apartment, but facing the memories of his old friend had been easy compared to handling Breanna.

"Tired?" Maggie asked as she sat in the recliner next to his chair and sipped at a cup of coffee.

"I'm beyond tired," he admitted, rubbing his bristled face with one hand, careful to slow his movements so as not to startle Breanna out of her doze. "I feel like I'm at least twice my age." At thirty, he'd considered himself in peak form, but that had been before Breanna had entered his life.

"You'll adjust," she predicted. "If my brothers could make the transformation to parenthood, so can you."

He purposely didn't point out that her brothers hadn't managed that feat on their own either. They'd had wives and the support of their families behind them. "If you say so. Regardless,

I've officially decided it's less stressful to work a thirty-six-hour shift than look after a baby."

"It'll get better."

He glanced at Maggie. "When?"

She smiled. "I'm sorry to disappoint you, but my crystal ball went the way of my time machine."

"I'll settle for a ballpark figure."

"How long does it take you to adjust to a new routine? A new house, new job, new friends? I'm guessing several weeks, minimum."

He hadn't thought of Breanna's situation in those terms and he should have. He'd grown up in foster-care and knew what it was like to be moved into a new home for reasons he often hadn't understood other than he couldn't stay where he'd been. Eventually, after he'd learned it didn't pay to get too cozy or too comfortable in any given residence because it didn't last, he began to consider his current placement as little more than a hotel.

"Of course, she's a baby, so she may make the transition sooner," she offered. "It's difficult to say."

"You're a ray of sunshine," he said dryly.

"That's what I'm here for," she said lightly. "To spread sunshine and good cheer."

Her smile brightened his spirits. "Speaking of sunshine, I don't want to think how this day would have gone if not for you. We wouldn't have accomplished a fraction of the things we did. It wouldn't surprise me if we'd still be at Hannah's, trying to get Breanna in my truck."

Breanna hadn't wanted to leave Hannah's place, and rightly so. Hannah was a familiar face in a now unfamiliar world and little Bee didn't want any part of her new life. Maggie, however, had taken charge. She'd matter-of-factly installed Breanna in the car seat and ignored her tantrum during the drive across town. Then, when they'd arrived at his house and he'd tried to carry her inside, Breanna had screamed blue murder until Maggie had simply said her name in the tone a school-teacher used on an unruly pupil. The little girl had instantly quieted.

"Oh, you'd have managed," she said lightly.

"I don't see how. And you kept her busy while I unloaded the furniture and assembled her crib." Even now, hours later, he could visualize the homey scene. Father working his magic with a screwdriver to assemble furniture while Mother and Baby watched, but he knew this picture's fairy-tale qualities were deceptive. Nothing lasted for ever. Not even cozy little family moments like the one he was now experiencing.

"I didn't do anything more than watch her play with her toys," she answered.

"Don't be so modest."

"OK, I'll take full credit for Breanna occupying herself." She stifled a yawn.

"Tired?" he asked.

"A little," she admitted.

"Busy night last night?" he asked, wishing he'd been part of whatever action they'd had.

"Not too bad. Our last call came in at midnight and after that, nothing."

"Until you got up early to make my soup."

"About that… You should have told the captain what was going on," she chided.

"Probably," he agreed. "But you wouldn't have landed on my doorstep with lunch in hand, would you?"

She smiled. "Probably not." She peered at Breanna's face. "I think she's asleep. Why don't you try putting her in her crib?"

Unfortunately, Maggie's suggestion didn't go smoothly. As he laid Breanna onto the mattress, the little girl instantly woke and began crying.

Nothing he did consoled her as she kicked out in her frustration.

Joe wanted to do the same. So much for hoping tonight would be different. Fortunately, the answer to his problems stood only a few feet away.

"What now?" he asked, his voice ragged as he hoisted Breanna out of her bed and onto his hip.

Maggie stared at the two standing before her, one weary, one unhappy. At that moment, she didn't know who tugged on her heartstrings more—the innocent whose life had been torn apart so easily by fate or the man who appeared so clearly powerless in the present circumstances. Tears of helplessness formed in her eyes, but she blinked them away. She had to remain strong and confident, not just for herself and for this little girl, but also for Joe. He was a man who thrived on being in control and at the moment he was fighting a losing battle against his feelings of inadequacy.

She held out her arms. "Let me have her."

He passed Breanna to her, but as he did so she saw the bleakness in his eyes and the expression of a man who knew he was completely out of his depth. Joe would need his confidence bolstered before she went home, but at the moment he had to wait his turn.

Maggie soothed the little one against her shoulder with every song she remembered. Fifteen minutes later, the cries were fading to hiccups.

She nuzzled Breanna's temple and inhaled her sweet baby scent as she told herself to remain detached. She simply had to rein in her feelings and not let them overrule her good sense. If she didn't, she'd be destroyed when she walked away. She could never lose sight of the fact that caring for Breanna was only a job, and a temporary one at that...

"Is she asleep?" she asked Joe.

He peeked. "Yeah. She's worn herself out."

Maggie was certain she appeared as haggard as Joe did. She certainly felt it. "I'll put her to bed, then."

As soon as Maggie returned from the bedroom, Joe was waiting for her. "I can't do this," he said flatly.

She understood completely. "Of course you can. She may be young, but she knows her mother isn't here. You just have to be patient until she learns that *you* are the stable factor in her life."

He shook his head. "No. I can't do it." He held out his hands. "Look at me. I'm shaking. If you hadn't been here—"

"But I was, Joe. Everything turned out fine."

"Right, now it did, but what about next time? I don't have what it takes."

"You're only lacking experience," she pointed out. "As you reminded me earlier today, my nieces and nephews have given me an advantage, but dealing with them as their aunt isn't the same as being a parent. I can spoil them rotten and then hand them back to my brothers."

"What about your boyfriend's kids?"

He would have to mention them. Thinking of Zach and Tyler, she added, "OK, so I took on a surrogate mother role for a while. It wasn't quite the same, though, because they still had their father as the one constant in their life. Still," she mused, "we had plenty of bad moments when the boys only wanted their mother, but they were too little to understand she wouldn't be coming home again. She'd died of cancer."

"I rest my case."

"The point is," she insisted, "you'll have rocky days and you'll have good ones, but you'll get through them. Now, if I were you," she said with a soft smile, "I'd grab some sleep. It's hard to say if she'll sense she's in a strange place and will wake up during the night so we can go through this again, or if she's so tuckered she'll sleep until morning. But never fear…" She moved to the coat closet where she'd hung her windbreaker. "I'll see you tomorrow, bright and early."

"You can't leave, Maggie," he said. "If she wakes up crying, you have to be here."

"If she wakes, change her diaper and heat another bottle. There are extras in the refrigerator, ready to go."

"You can't leave," he repeated. "I can't comfort her like you just did and that's what she needs."

She understood his fear but it only proved that Joe had more fatherly qualities than he wanted to admit. If he'd truly been uncaring, she would have seen something other than worry in his eyes—something like irritation or anger perhaps, not concern or fear that he couldn't meet Breanna's needs. "You'll do fine."

"Please, Maggie? I'm begging you. For tonight."

She wanted to refuse in order to protect herself, to use distance to help her stay emotionally detached.

"You can have my bed," he said. "I'll sleep on the couch."

"This isn't a good idea," she began.

"If she wakes up, I'm calling you," he warned,

"regardless of the time. If you don't come over, we'll drive to your place."

She wanted to run away as much as Joe wanted her to stay because she already knew she would have a difficult time leaving this precious baby in a few weeks. How could she not? A motherless baby was bound to tug on a childless woman's heart, especially after she'd already lost two children she'd once thought of as her own.

"You have to start dealing with her some time, Donatelli."

"I know and I will. Just not tonight. Please?"

Certain she wouldn't relax if she went home anyway because she'd spend what was left of the night wondering what Joe was doing and how he was coping, she gave in. "OK. I'll run home and grab a few clothes—"

"What's mine is yours," he said. "T-shirts, sweatpants, jeans, whatever. I'll even lend you my razor if you want it."

Knowing how her brothers always complained if their wives dulled the blades, she quipped, "The supreme sacrifice."

A smile tugged at the corners of his mouth and his deer-in-the-headlights look eased. "How about it, partner?"

She thought about all the chores she'd planned to do on her day off and decided these two needed her more than her dust bunnies did. "Only if I can go home after breakfast tomorrow."

He stepped forward and hugged her. "Thanks, Maggie. This means a lot to me."

Maggie had never allowed herself to imagine what it would feel like to be in Joe's arms. It would only have led to problems, but now that she was where she'd occasionally allowed herself to fantasize, she had to admit this spot was quite satisfying. Heady, in fact.

She noticed the strength in his biceps, felt his heartbeat against her cheek, breathed in his unique scent, a blend of Joe Donatelli and soap, and realized something unexpected.

Breanna wasn't the only person capable of breaking her heart. Without any effort at all, Joe could do the same.

After his shower the next morning, Joe hesitated on the kitchen threshold to watch the two girls who'd entered his life without warning, one wearing a fuzzy pink sleeper and the other still wearing the clothes he'd given her after he'd talked her into staying the night. He'd never be able to wear that particular pair of sweatpants and long-sleeved T-shirt again without remembering how both had hinted at the curves they had concealed. Heaven help him when he saw her wearing shorts or a swimsuit!

Determined to keep his thoughts under control, he gratefully noticed Maggie had already brewed a pot of coffee and was feeding Breanna breakfast, although the youngster was more intent on trying to feed herself. With careful deliberation, the little girl picked up a single Cheerio, popped it into her mouth and chewed it with a noisy crunch before she repeated the process. After five carefully eaten Cheerios, she grabbed her sippy cup and took a long drink before allowing Maggie to spoon something orange—strained peaches?—into her mouth.

He headed directly to the coffee and poured a mug for himself. "Good morning, ladies. How did you sleep?"

"Great. Like a log," Maggie answered cheerfully from her place at the table. "Your bed is really comfortable."

He grinned. "I like to think so."

"No one else has told you that?"

Joe was quite aware of his reputation. The guys

at the station teased him mercilessly about his love life and rather than admit he didn't have any or that he limited his encounters to women who weren't interested in more than a few nights of no-strings companionship, he played along with their assumptions that he lived his bachelorhood to the fullest. Oh, he didn't live a celibate life, but he'd always gone to the woman's apartment so he could leave whenever he pleased. His home was his private domain—his sanctuary—and he didn't share it with just anyone.

"No," he said.

She stared at him incredulously. "Are you telling me—?"

"You're the only woman who's slept in that bed. Contrary to public opinion, I don't bring my dates here. Ever. For any reason."

"Not even for coffee?"

"For any reason," he repeated.

Approval lit up her face—approval that he hadn't realized how badly he wanted from her until she gave it. "A wise decision, considering Breanna's in your life now. So…" She drew out in a tone that heralded a conversation shift. "How was the sofa?"

"OK." What could he say? It was a sofa and

while it worked well for a Sunday afternoon nap, it lacked a lot in the good-night's-sleep department.

If the too-short frame that didn't accommodate his form wasn't enough, a host of other issues had cluttered his mind. Worries about fatherhood and the responsibilities associated with it, the multitude of decisions to be made and details to be organized and his own fears marched through his head with staccato-like precision.

When he'd finally been able to convince himself that those concerns had to wait until morning, a mental picture of Maggie tangled in *his* sheets, wearing *his* T-shirt and her lacy underwear made him break out in a sweat.

He'd finally dozed off in the wee hours, knowing that Maggie would come running if Breanna awoke. He wouldn't have had any rest at all if Maggie hadn't given him peace of mind.

Although he faced a host of frightening challenges today as they all settled into a new routine, he felt more able to cope with Maggie nearby. Unfortunately, as comforting as it was to know he could depend on her to get him through today, his child-care problems had to be solved soon. They were scheduled to work tomorrow and he didn't have any idea what he was going to do with Breanna. It wasn't as if he could take her to the station with him, but knowing how difficult this whole situation was for his daughter—*presumably* his daughter—he hated the idea of putting the squirt through another night like last night where she was left once again with strangers.

Where *did* someone take their child when twenty-four-hour care was necessary?

Hell, maybe he should just call the captain and beg for more vacation time. Idly, he wondered what it would cost him to talk Maggie into doing the same because the idea of spending another entire day on his own was a grim one.

As he glanced at her and saw her delicate brow raised inquisitively, he knew he'd zoned out her question.

"Sorry," he said, embarrassed she'd caught him daydreaming. "You were saying?"

"I asked if you were rested and refreshed."

He took mental stock of his body's aches and pains. "More or less. Why? What do you have planned?"

Her smile slowly spread across her face. "A field trip."

Immediately, he wondered about the logistics of taking an eleven-month-old anywhere. "Where?"

"To my friend's house."

Paying social calls wasn't on his schedule. At all. "Any particular reason why we're visiting?" he asked gruffly. "I'd hoped we'd spend the day finding sitters for Breanna. She has to go somewhere tomorrow."

"I know she does, but I'm not aware of any place nearby that is licensed to keep a child for twenty-four hours at a time. The way I see it, you need an at-home care provider."

"And where do I find one of those? On short notice?"

She smiled. "Today is your lucky day because that's where we're going—to find you a sitter. My friend, Nancy, just moved back to Barton Hills after living in New York for the past several years. She was a nanny for a bank executive until the economy tanked and he lost his job.

"Anyway," she continued, "Nancy's looking for another position. I didn't know if she'd be interested in taking care of Breanna because you won't need her every day, but I took the liberty of calling her early this morning."

This was more than good news. It was *excel-*

lent news—news that exceeded his wildest dreams. "And?" he demanded, half-afraid to hope for the best.

She grinned. "Nancy wants to meet you before she'll commit, and of course she wants more details about our work schedule and your expectations. As she's living at home to help her parents remodel, she seemed to like the idea that she'd have more days to herself."

"She's reliable?"

"She worked for the same couple for five years and left with a glowing recommendation in her pocket. I'll warn you, though. She doesn't come cheap and she's choosy about her employers."

At this point, he would pay anything to solve Breanna's child-care problems. "*I'm* the one on trial?" he asked wryly.

"I wouldn't worry too much. I'll convince her you're a decent sort." She grinned.

In light of everything that had happened between them, he was awed by her willingness to help him. "You'd do that? For me?"

"Sure. Why not? We're partners, remember?" she finished lightly.

Partners. In this one act, Maggie had given new meaning to the word. He stared at her, hardly able to believe his luck. No, Lady Luck wasn't involved, unless her name was Maggie. Once again, he thanked the Fates for pairing them.

"Aren't you going to say something?" she demanded. "If you don't want to take her there, just say—"

"Not want to?" he asked as the weight on his shoulders suddenly lifted. "Of course I do."

The concern on her face turned to suspicion. "You don't seem too happy about it. Honestly, if you want to make other arrangements, you won't hurt my feelings."

"I don't want other arrangements," he said, "and, yes, I'm happy. Deliriously happy. So happy, in fact…" He didn't give himself time to think about what he was doing, or time to talk himself out of it. He only acted.

He set his mug on the counter, pulled her close and kissed her.

It was supposed to be a simple way of saying thanks—a swift brush of their lips—but once his mouth met hers, his initial intentions fled. After token resistance, she melted against him and only one thought ran through his fevered brain.

This was what he needed. After facing the past he'd buried long ago and dealing with a present that had forced him to fight his demons in a battle he still hadn't won, kissing Maggie brought him back to life.

Oh, how he wanted to live!

His arms tightened and he greedily consumed her mouth, aware that she responded in kind. No shrinking violet, this Maggie, no half-measures, just pure and honest response. Dimly, he noted her arms wrapping around his neck as they stood with their bodies pressed full length against each other.

He'd kissed other women before, but none of them compared to Maggie. Each feathery stroke of her fingers generated so much heat that he was certain his body temperature had reached a crisis point.

In the background, he heard Breanna banging her cup against the highchair tray as she raised her voice over her own din. He'd been with her long enough to recognize when she was finished eating and would soon be bored. He had a minute at most before she would arch her back and try to escape on her own if left to her own devices.

Slowly, reluctantly, he loosened his hold as necessity demanded, but more than a few inches of distance was impossible. Right now, he couldn't move; his heart still raced from the adrenalin rush and his breath was ragged.

"We shouldn't have done that," she said in a voice holding the same breathless quality as his.

"Probably not." But, oh, he was glad that they had. Knowledge was power and he felt extremely powerful.

"We can't do it again."

He raised an eyebrow. "Why not?"

She stared at him as if he had grown an extra eye in the middle of his forehead. "Because it causes extra problems and we have enough on our hands at the moment."

He liked the way she included herself in the problems facing him. *We.* He'd never been part of a 'we' before. Then again, he'd never *allowed* anyone to be a part of his life because in the end everyone left.

She continued, "We work together, remember? Fraternization is frowned on."

"Only if it violates the chain of command," he said, taking the temperature of this relationship to see if Maggie wanted it to go anywhere, at least temporarily. "As we're both equals, I'm not your supervisor and you aren't mine, so whatever we do wouldn't pose a problem. And our partnership is only temporary. As soon as Robert gets cleared for work, I'll be going back to Station Two."

"It's still frowned on," she insisted. "We both work the same shift, sleep in the same common room, even if we have a dozen chaperones. The department can't afford to have any rumors of impropriety circulating."

Damn! Unfortunately, she had a point. They couldn't let their hormones lead them around by the nose, although he disagreed with her reason. The 'work' factor could be dealt with because the roadblock to their relationship would be removed in a few months. However, the real case against a relationship was that he couldn't handle long term and from the few details he'd gleaned about her past relationships, Maggie was unlikely to settle for anything less.

"It was only a kiss, Maggie." Even if he wanted it to be more.

"As long as we both understand that."

"Sure. Whatever you say." But as he watched her reach out and smooth Breanna's hair before tickling the little girl under her chin, he wondered if Maggie had been trying to convince herself as much as she'd tried to convince him.

"Speaking of the department," she began slowly, her expression pensive, "I wonder if leaving Breanna with a sitter so soon after she's moved in with you is a good idea. Maybe you should take tomorrow off? In fact, you should ask for an entire week. Captain will understand."

"We're short-handed," he reminded her.

"We can pull one of the emergency medical technician firemen to ride with me," she said. "Last shift I worked with Kevin Running Bear."

He didn't like the idea of leaving the department in the lurch. He'd made a personal vow to be dependable and calling in on such short notice didn't sit well with him. On the flip side, though, he had Breanna to consider. It didn't seem right for him to disappear so soon after he'd walked into her life. Already he felt the squeeze of choosing between the responsibilities of his career with those of Dee's daughter. He suddenly developed new respect for the men who managed to juggle both, although those same men with children also had wives or partners to share the load.

"Little Bee will be better off spending the day with your friend, the nanny," he stated firmly.

"She needs to grow accustomed to *you* before you introduce her to someone else new."

"In an ideal situation, yes, but we both know this isn't ideal," he said flatly. "Besides, who knows how long it might take for her to realize I'm one of the good guys? You said yourself we couldn't put a timeframe on her getting acclimated to me. It could happen today and it might take months. I can't put my life on hold indefinitely."

"Maybe not, but she certainly needs more than two days."

As he saw the frown on Maggie's face, he conceded. "OK, I'll talk to the Captain, but I won't put an extra burden on the department."

"But you will call him?" she pressed.

"I will," he promised. With luck, Captain Keller would need him on duty and he could have a normal day in the middle of the chaos his life had become.

"Great." She headed for the hallway. "You two have fun while I take my turn in the bathroom."

He wanted to protest, but he couldn't demand that she never leave him alone with Breanna. Instead, he watched her disappear, heard her feet pad down the hall until the bathroom door clicked in the distance. Fortunately, her honeysuckle fragrance remained to remind him that he wasn't the only adult in the house.

"OK, kid," he said as he eyed the little girl. "It's you and me."

Breanna looked at him. "Mama?"

The hope in her voice made him feel completely inadequate. "Mama's gone," he said softly, reaching out to stroke her fine curls. "I'm here."

Apparently satisfied that he would fill the gap, at least temporarily, she raised her arms and wiggled, her signal that she wanted to be picked up.

After a few struggles with the tray latch, he extricated her from the highchair and carried her into the living room where he held her on his lap. Immediately, she squirmed and he set her on the floor, next to the laundry basket containing her toys.

For the next fifteen minutes he watched her as she squeezed her squeaky toys, chewed on others, and played with some contraption that made various animal noises when he pulled the string. By the time Maggie returned, he'd been so intent on watching over the little girl so she didn't hurt herself on anything that he felt as if he'd gone ten rounds with a prizefighter.

"How are you two doing?" she asked.

"No blood, no bruises and no tears, so I guess we did OK." It was ridiculous how relieved he was to see her, even though she'd only been a few feet away. How would he manage if she ever left them alone for hours? Or, worse yet, an entire day?

CHAPTER FOUR

"MAGGIE, a word, please."

At Captain Keller's command, Maggie looked up from her task of disinfecting their ambulance equipment after their last call involving a formerly spry eighty-year-old woman who'd tripped over another resident's cane at a nearby nursing home and broken her hip. The old gal couldn't have weighed more than her age and she'd barely made a wrinkle in their sheets, but protocol was still protocol.

She clambered out of the back of the ambulance to find her boss waiting for her, his expression serious. "Sir," she acknowledged cautiously. "What's up?"

Keller motioned her to the opposite of the ambulance where they wouldn't be visible to anyone passing by. "Watch Joe's back today, will you?"

She studied her superior, surprised by his

request. "Sure, but that's something we *always* do," she pointed out tactfully. She didn't mention that this unwritten rule had caused friction between the two of them in the first place. Joe had watched her a bit too closely and found fault with everything she'd done while she'd become defensive and suspicious, but that was in the past and she hoped they'd turned a new page.

"I know, but if he looks like he's not able to function, let me know."

"OK," she said cautiously, surprised that the captain, who normally frowned on telling tales on coworkers, was apparently breaking his own rule.

"As you're aware, he's under a lot of stress right now," he continued. "I would have given him the day off, not to mention rushed through an emergency paternity leave, but…" he shook his head "…with so many people on medical waivers and one person gone for arson training, I'm in dire straits."

"So he said." Joe had relayed his conversation with Keller yesterday and although he hadn't expressed his relief about being needed on duty, Maggie sensed that he was pleased to be back on familiar ground. Yet, while it was less than ideal for both Breanna's and Joe's adjustment, Maggie understood the captain's position. In her opinion, though, this was a no-win situation for everyone.

"I know he's going through a rough patch with this baby," he continued. "A man who can count his hours of sleep on one hand over the last seventy-two hours isn't functioning at peak efficiency. I'm counting on you to be extra-vigilant."

"I will."

"And if you see something…"

"I'll tell you," she promised, although she wondered what he'd do if she *did* catch Joe making a mistake. Would he send Joe home? Talk to him? Demand that Maggie act as the senior paramedic for every case?

However, worrying over the captain's decision on a non-event was pointless. The patients were her concern and they would remain so, regardless of Joe's personal issues.

As she turned away, Keller stopped her. "Oh, and, Maggie?" She paused. "Joe told me what you're doing to help him out."

"He did? I'm surprised."

"In fact, he called you a godsend." Keller's serious expression suddenly became jovial. "Quite a change in a few days."

"Yeah, well, if it weren't for your lecture, I

wouldn't have gotten embroiled in his family problems in the first place," she said wryly. "But I want you to know I'm only doing this because he's my partner. And he's helpless around kids. I couldn't leave him to muddle through on his own."

She'd wanted to. Still did, in fact, but she'd agreed to help him and that was that.

"I know this isn't easy for you," he began.

"You can say that again," she said fervently.

"Does he know about Arthur and the boys?"

"He's heard the basics."

His eyebrows furrowed slightly. "As glad as I am to have you two working together like a team instead of sniping at each other, I also don't want you to crash and burn like you did last time."

After Arthur had left town with Zach and Tyler, she'd done her best to carry on as if her world hadn't fallen apart. She'd been reasonably certain she'd hidden the worst from the guys at the station but apparently she'd been wrong. Those nights when she'd roamed the dark hallways because she couldn't sleep, those times when she'd stiffened as someone mentioned their kids' antics or recited a funny story, those mornings when she'd got up with her eyes weary and bloodshot instead of bright and sparkly, obviously hadn't gone unnoticed.

"I won't," she promised. "The situations are totally different. Helping him with Breanna is like helping my brothers with their kids. Good old Aunt Maggie to the rescue."

He nodded, seemingly satisfied by her answer. "I'm glad to hear it. Meanwhile, if there's anything the rest of us can do for Joe, let me know."

"I will." Yet, as she went back to work, she knew she'd only been lying to her captain. Helping Joe *wasn't* the same as helping her family because her thoughts concerning her partner weren't brotherly at all. His kisses were too potent to even remotely put him in the same category.

As she returned to her task, two more firemen, Gary Shepherd and Jim Bowman, affectionately known as Shep and Jimbo, stuck their heads in the back of the ambulance. "Yo, Maggie. Do you have a minute?"

She paused once again. "Only until Joe gets back."

"He'll be a while. The lieutenant has him looking up some report."

"Then what can I do for you?"

"Is the story true? He's got a kid?" Jimbo asked.

"Who told you?"

"No one. We overheard him talking to the Captain."

Maggie chose to carefully edit Joe's story. If he wanted to give specifics and more details, he could do it himself.

"He does," she agreed as she sprayed, then wiped down the gurney railings. "Remember the lady whose car slid into the tree? She was a friend of Joe's. Being a single mom, she'd appointed Joe as her daughter's legal guardian if anything ever happened to her."

"So now he's a daddy." Shep shook his head. "Man, oh, man. Poor dude. I know how petrified I was with our first one and I had nine months to get used to the idea before we brought her home. It has to be worse for Joe, being a single guy and all."

Jimbo nodded. "It'll definitely cramp his style."

Maggie concentrated on cleaning the stainless-steel surfaces. She wouldn't ruin Joe's reputation as a ladies' man. If he wanted to admit he spent most evenings alone, that was his secret to divulge, not hers.

"Nah, it won't," Shep said, sounding like the forty-eight-year-old voice of experience that he was. "Women flock to single fathers. It's all part of that nurturing, nesting instinct they have. He'll be married within the year, mark my words."

The idea stung, although it shouldn't. Their off-duty relationship revolved only around Breanna. If not for the little girl, they wouldn't even *have* an off-duty relationship. But Breanna or not, this arrangement would only last for a few weeks.

"Whatever happens, he'll need your support," she said. "He's feeling overwhelmed right now."

Both men nodded. "Understandable."

Shep's gaze landed on her. "You're his partner. Are you giving him a hand?"

It was an unspoken rule—partners covered for each other, followed by the rest of the shift's crew, then the entire department. Letting her "other half" bear a burden alone was like a betrayal of their code of honor. But even if she wanted to minimize her role because of the potential for ugly gossip, she couldn't deny the truth—everyone would eventually discover it.

"He's asked me to help him for a few weeks," she admitted, "until he gets his feet wet." She purposely kept the paternity-test issue to herself. That information was also Joe's to share, not hers. "It seemed the least I could do."

Satisfaction appeared on Shep's lean face. She

got the distinct impression that he approved, and if he approved, no one else would dare argue with the most senior firefighter on their crew. "Yeah. You're perfect for the job. If you ask me, this shows there's a Man Upstairs orchestrating behind the scenes. Heaven help Donatelli if he'd gotten stuck with Klaxton as his partner."

George Klaxton was a nice enough fellow, but he had problems. Financial, marital, family—it didn't matter. He moved from one crisis to another and as such, needed more support from his coworkers than he gave. He wouldn't have been much help to Joe except to share horror stories and drag him to bars so they could cry in their beers together.

The two men moved off, but oddly enough Shep's comment about marriage burrowed under her skin. Why, she didn't know. Their kiss hadn't been a declaration of romance, or implied any interest on his part. Joe had simply gotten carried away with his gratitude.

As for the way it had knocked her sideways, she could only claim celibacy as her excuse. She'd been telling herself to start dating again, but she'd dragged her feet. Her response to his kiss was a simple case of her hormones reminding her that she was a woman and he was an attractive man.

"Squad Two. Engine Two," the dispatcher announced over the intercom. "Respond to a single-vehicle accident with a train at the railroad crossing of McKinley and Pine. Be advised injuries are reported."

Immediately Maggie sprang into action, shoving aside her cleaning supplies before she jumped out the back and latched the double doors. As she slid into the driver's seat—it was Joe's turn to ride shotgun—he came tearing into the vehicle bay with the rest of the crew. Within seconds, they were on their way.

Exactly eight minutes later they arrived at the intersection in question to see a red compact car crumpled beside the railroad tracks, apparently having been dragged several hundred feet by the impact with the train's engine. Two police cruisers were parked nearby, their lights blazing. The officers were huddled around the wrecked vehicle and a small group of bystanders had gathered a short distance away.

"It doesn't look good from here," Maggie said tersely as she braked hard near the scene, aware of the fire truck pulling up beside her. "Are there two people in that car?"

"Looks like only one," Joe said as he unlatched

his seat belt before he opened his door, "which is one too many. Trains and cars just don't mix." While he grabbed the medical kit from the back of their ambulance, Maggie retrieved the backboards.

"The driver has been unconscious since I arrived," the officer directing traffic told them as they approached. "She's now responding, but she isn't doing well."

"Thanks," Joe said. "We'll take it from here."

The officer moved away while Joe took his place next to the victim. Maggie stood beside him, noting the woman's bruised face, the small trickle of blood out of her nose and mouth.

"Ma'am," he began, "we're from the fire department and we're here to help you. Can you tell me where it hurts?"

The woman moved her mouth, but nothing came out. Joe repeated his question as Maggie watched him check her pulse and respirations.

"My...head," the woman managed to say.

"Don't worry," Joe told her, "we'll get you to the hospital."

"My...daughter."

Joe visibly stiffened. Clearly he was experiencing déjà vu. "Your daughter?"

"She's...at...dance class. Pick...her up. Late."

The relief in Joe's eyes was clear as he glanced at Maggie. "Let's get her immobilized and out of there."

Minutes later, the rest of the fire crew was swarming the vehicle. "Status report?" Captain Keller asked briskly.

Joe answered. "We've got to get her out fast," he said in a low, worried voice. "We'll need the Hurst equipment."

Keller nodded. "OK, then. Get her ready," he said, referring to the victim.

But as Maggie was helping Joe position the protective tarp to cover them from any possible flying debris, the woman's head fell lifelessly to one side.

Joe muttered an expletive that Maggie silently echoed as he checked her carotid pulse. "Hurry up," he yelled at the men surrounding them. "We've got to get her out of there *now!*"

Although Shep and the rest of the crew worked efficiently, each second seemed to last an hour as they revved up the jaws of life to pop apart the twisted metal and extract the victim. At long last they were lifting her away from the shell of the car and strapping her to the gurney.

"We have an ID," one of the officers came alongside them to announce. "Angela Merton.

Her husband's been notified and he'll meet you at the hospital."

In a corner of her brain Maggie noted the name, but the woman's condition was deteriorating before their eyes.

"We're losing her," Joe said tersely as he bent over the gurney while Maggie and three others carried her to the ambulance. "As soon as I insert an airway, let's go."

Maggie slid behind the wheel and prepared to press on the gas pedal once Joe gave the word.

"Ready," he yelled.

Maggie called in their ETA as she raced to the hospital in what seemed like record time. When they arrived, a trauma team stood on the ambulance bay dock, ready to take over as Joe gave his report.

"I hope this isn't an indication of how our day will go," Maggie commented later, still feeling jittery from her adrenaline high as they wheeled their now-empty stretcher past the lounge to the exit.

"Yeah. Me, too. Do you mind if we stop for a cup of coffee? I can use one."

"I thought you'd never ask."

But before they could detour to the ever-ready

urn, their radio squawked and the dispatcher sent them on another call.

"No rest for the wicked," Maggie quipped as Joe helped her load the gurney before they sped toward a home with a potential heart attack patient.

Forty minutes after that they were back at the hospital, delivering a fifty-nine-year-old man for a cardiac evaluation.

On their way once again to the ambulance, the same ER physician who'd received Angela Merton passed them in the hall.

"How's the car-crash victim?" Joe asked. "The lady with the head injuries?"

The doctor shook his head and shrugged wearily. "There was nothing we could do."

Joe's expression fell. "I see. Thanks, Doc."

Maggie sensed Joe's withdrawal. "What a tragedy," she murmured.

"Yeah, it's too bad. I wonder what Shep's fixing for dinner?" he asked.

Maggie stared at him incredulously. They'd just lost a patient and he was worried about *lunch?* But as she opened her mouth to scold him, she noticed the grim set to his mouth and the slump to his shoulders, as if the death of this woman had affected him more than he cared to admit.

Surreptitiously, she studied him as they trudged back to the ambulance. It was humbling to realize that during the three weeks they'd been paired together, she'd never looked beyond his placid expression and quiet demeanor to the emotions below. At first glance, and even second, he'd always appeared cool, unflappable, and as steady and emotionless as a rock.

Idly, she wondered if everyone else had fallen into the same trap of seeing only what he wanted them to see. She'd initially thought him cold-hearted and distant, but the events of the past two days had proven her wrong—he was simply a master at hiding his deepest emotions in order to protect his tender heart.

Joe's first day back on the job hadn't been so busy that he felt as if he and Maggie were run ragged but busy enough that he hadn't found time to dwell on his personal life. However, as the night deepened and he lay on his bunk and listened to the gentle snores of those sharing the common sleeping area, the memories he'd held at bay all came to the forefront of his mind.

Look after the baby. You're all she has... Promise.

Dee's request tumbled over in his head,

making it impossible to rest. He grabbed his ever-ready flashlight and padded to the basement where he planned to wear himself out with exercise until he was simply too tired to think.

As he walked into the musty weight room and stripped off his Barton Hills fire department sweatshirt to the T-shirt underneath, he wished he had a "cooking" stress reliever plan like Maggie did, because then he'd have something to show for his sleeplessness besides sore muscles and sweat-drenched clothes. He'd heard tales of how the guys woke up in the morning with the scent of freshly baked cinnamon rolls wafting through the station and right now nothing sounded better than home-made comfort food.

But bench presses were all he had, so he started his routine. When he'd finished, he started again. An hour later, he was hot and sweaty and physically exhausted, but he couldn't face his bed just yet. Not with Maggie lying on the other side of a half-partition as a politically correct concession to her gender. He'd worked with only a handful of women over the years, but he'd never been attracted to them to the degree that he was toward Maggie. She made him feel emotions he hadn't ever felt as well as made him wish for the impossible, which was probably why he'd tried to find reasons *not* to like her.

At least, he had until now.

A softly spoken "Can't sleep?" caught him by surprise. Nearly dropping a forty-pound free weight on his foot, he cursed. "Hell, Maggie. You scared the sh—crap out of me. What are you doing up at this hour?"

She padded in, wearing the same department-issue sweats that he was, although as a concession to the hot-blooded guys who turned down the air-conditioning to near-frigid levels, she was wearing a hooded sweatshirt instead of a T. "I could ask you the same thing."

"Don't. Just go back to bed."

"No can do. I wouldn't be much of a partner if I ignored you when you were hurting."

"I'm fine."

She rolled her eyes. "Don't insult my intelligence, Joe. You can pretend to be this unfeeling fellow to the rest of the world, but not to me. We're partners. If you can't be honest with me, who can you be honest with?"

He hesitated. "True."

"Mrs Merton's death reminded you of Dee's."

He couldn't deny it. "In a way."

"And it bothers you."

"A little," he prevaricated, aware of how his admission went contrary to the lecture he'd given her over Hilda Myers. "I suppose next you'll rub my nose in how unobjective I'm being."

At first she didn't answer. "I would have thought by now you'd know me better than that," she chided gently. "Some accidents have a bigger impact on us than others. You've surely had patients who tugged at your heart before now. Patients who, for whatever reason, reminded you of a family member you loved?"

He'd thought of the drunks he'd hauled to the hospital, the men who'd thought the answer to everything lay in their fists. Oh, he'd seen plenty of men like his father, but no one in the loving category she described. Except for Dee. "No."

She blinked. "No one?"

"No one," he said firmly.

"Not even a little bit?" She pinched her fingers together in the air.

"No."

"Gee, Joe. You give new meaning to the word 'detached.'" She sounded exasperated.

He'd always been careful not to let himself get too close to anyone. Some might say he was cold, but it was safer that way. "Emotions interfere with our objectivity, and then we become less effective in the field."

"So you've said before. And yet Dee was different—the exception to your rule."

His deep sigh seemed to originate in his feet. "She was."

"As painful as it is for you to lose a friend, if you didn't feel something, I'd really worry about you."

The concept of someone worrying about him was foreign and made him uncomfortable. Then again, it was more disconcerting to be alone with her in a room where a padded mat lay in the corner as he saw her long curly hair hanging in disarray around her face, being painfully aware of how her sweatsuit didn't completely disguise her soft curves. He swiped the perspiration off his face with a hand towel, wishing women hadn't been allowed to enter this profession.

Not all women, he corrected himself. Only Maggie. Thanks to his job, she was the one woman he shouldn't have as long as they worked together, regardless of how much she stirred him in ways he shouldn't be stirred.

"Tell me about her," she said as she straddled another weight bench.

After being paired alongside Maggie for three weeks, he'd learned one thing. She was like a pit-bull fighting over a bone when she wanted information. "There's really not much to tell," he prevaricated.

"Of course there is. What brought you two together in the first place?"

"Do you really want to know?"

"Of course. We're partners, remember? If it will make you feel better, whatever you say in this room stays in this room. I don't kiss and tell."

He mentally groaned, wishing she hadn't said the word *kiss*. It reminded him of the one they'd shared yesterday—the one he'd like to repeat, but couldn't. At least, not here in the station where it could spell suicide for his career if he was caught. As being a paramedic *was* his life, he couldn't foolishly jeopardize it just to scratch a temporary itch, regardless of how intense that itch was.

Wanting her to leave for his peace of mind and knowing she wouldn't until she got what she came for, he capitulated. He placed the weight back on its stand, straddled a bench and swiped his face again with his towel. "What do you want to know?" he asked wearily.

"How did you meet? Did you know her long? Did she make you laugh, that sort of thing?"

"She was an evening shift waitress at the restaurant near the apartment I had. I'd drop in for a piece of pie late at night and we'd talk. After I learned she lived in a housing complex not far from me, I started walking her home."

After a few such nights she'd invited him to stay for breakfast, and he had, but it seemed tacky to share that detail, especially with a woman he'd love to see across his own breakfast table.

"What was she like?"

"Quiet. Smiled a lot, but didn't say much. She was taking a court reporter course. She grew up in foster-care like I did." He didn't know why he tacked on that last piece of information, but it seemed important for Maggie to understand their shared background had been the glue that had cemented their friendship.

"When did you see her last?"

"I moved out of the neighborhood not quite a year and a half ago. Haven't seen or heard from her since." He paused. "I still can't believe she named me as Breanna's father.

Shouldn't she have *told* me if little Bee was mine? Truly *mine?*"

Maggie shrugged. "She obviously had her reasons for doing what she did."

"I wish I knew what they were." In spite of Dee's desire to have a houseful of kids, he'd always been adamant that parenting wasn't an option for him because he wouldn't risk repeating his father's mistakes. Why Dee would circumvent his express wish was a mystery he wanted solved. The only logical explanation was that Breanna was in fact, his, that their birth control had failed as a result of a freak cosmic joke, but he refused to accept the possibility.

"But you still believe some other fellow was in the picture?"

"I'm sure of it," he said flatly. "And I intend to find him, if I can."

"I wish you luck with your quest, Joe." She stifled a yawn. "Meanwhile, the only thing I want to find is my pillow so I can hit the hay before the alarm goes off. Are you coming, or do you need a mug of hot chocolate first?"

Her invitation to return to their respective beds was innocent but, oh, how he wished it weren't!

If Maggie knew the direction of his thoughts, she'd probably bar him from the room.

"I'm coming." He followed her to the door, his towel slung around his neck.

In the hallway, she turned abruptly to face him and he nearly barreled into her. "A piece of advice, Donatelli."

"What's that?"

She wrinkled her nose. "Hit the shower before you bunk down. The guys will dream about skunks invading the station if you don't." Her wide grin softened her uncomplimentary comment.

A chuckle worked its way out of his throat. "You don't care for the locker-room smell?"

"Not when I'm trying to sleep."

He faked a long-suffering sigh. "OK. Anything to make my partner happy…"

She sauntered off with a smile that lingered in his memory until he'd finally settled into his bunk. It was a smile that he'd never tire of seeing and one he'd never forget.

CHAPTER FIVE

THE report of a warehouse fire in the manufacturing district woke Maggie out of a sound sleep at 4:00 a.m. and sent her entire station crew to the scene. Although she and Joe had begun their careers as firefighters, the Barton Hills Fire Department was staffed with enough personnel so the paramedics could stand by to do what they did best. Firefighting was hard, dirty work, and although the staff was well trained, not everyone returned to the station unscathed. Minor burns, smoke inhalation and falls were only a few of the conditions Maggie had treated during her tenure.

Barring anything serious, her job—and Joe's—was to ensure that the men remained hydrated and allowed themselves enough of a break to recover from their activities before they returned to the action. At the moment Maggie was watching the first streaks of dawn appear in the sky as she leaned against the ambulance's front bumper.

"I feel guilty just standing and watching while everyone else is working their tails off," she commented to Joe. "Especially during the winter months when it's cold."

"Don't feel too guilty," he said before he glanced at his wrist. "Shep and Jimbo will be paying us a visit before long. They're on their second oxygen bottle and by my watch, they're both almost out of air. After that, we'll be hard-pressed to keep up."

As each man was allowed two thirty-minute bottles of oxygen, which lasted about fifteen to twenty minutes under strenuous activity, they would be rotating out of the line for rehab. Then, as Joe had said, they would both be busy until their colleagues controlled the fire.

Joe's prediction came true minutes later. The two men he'd mentioned trudged to the ambulance, reeking of smoke and breathing hard as sweat trickled down their sooty faces.

"How are you guys doing?" she asked as she ushered them inside the back of the vehicle and helped Shep remove his coat while Joe did the same for Jimbo.

"Helluva way to wake up," Shep stated.

"Yeah, but that's why we get paid the big bucks," Jimbo quipped facetiously.

"Yeah, but I was in the middle of a great dream," Shep groused good-naturedly as he held out his hand while Maggie clipped the pulse oximeter to a finger. "I was sitting in my boat in the middle of the lake and the fish were biting as fast as I threw in my line."

"You *were* dreaming, weren't you?" she teased.

"I'll say. I was in the middle of landing a beauty," he mourned. "Now I'll never know if I caught him or not."

She quickly took Shep's vital signs. His pulse rate was elevated, which was to be expected. So was his blood pressure, but only marginally, and his oxygen saturation level remained high. After a short break to drink a bottle of water, she released him for duty, while Joe did the same for Jimbo.

The firefighters all rotated through med rehab, one after another, until the warehouse was reduced to a pile of smoldering embers. Just when Maggie was certain they were going to wrap up the operation and head back to the station, there was a flurry of activity at the far end of the property.

Joe's two-way radio squawked before the

captain's voice came through. "Man injured. Squad Two, stand by."

Maggie glanced at Joe. "I wonder what happened?"

"We'll find out soon enough," he said grimly. "But from the looks of things..." he gazed across the lot "...it can't be too bad if our patient is walking."

A few yards away, Jimbo was supporting a white-faced Shep as they ambled toward them.

Maggie rushed to Shep's side and helped support him the remaining few steps to the ambulance. "What happened?"

"I tripped. Fell on my arm," Shep managed to say as he sank onto the gurney that Joe had fashioned into a chair so he could sit upright. "Can't raise my arm. Hurts like the dickens. Feels like the last time I dislocated my shoulder."

Maggie opened his clothing and saw an obvious deformity.

"I think you're right," she told him, "but we'll let the doctor decide."

Muttering several choice expletives, Shep closed his eyes and leaned against the mattress as Maggie splinted his arm so as not to jar the bones during transport.

At the hospital, the doctor agreed. "We'll get X-rays just to be sure," he said, "and then we'll reduce the dislocation. Shouldn't take too long if you guys want to stick around and take him back with you."

"We'll wait," Joe decided. "We need to pick up a few supplies anyway."

"I'll have one of the nurses let you know when we're finished."

Clearly dismissed, Maggie followed Joe into the hallway. "Do you have the supply list on you or shall I run out and get it?"

Joe grabbed her arm and steered her toward the elevators. "It's in my pocket, but we're going to have breakfast first."

"Hungry, eh?" she teased.

"Starving," he answered. "And today is waffle day."

"I didn't know you liked waffles."

He grinned. "You'll find I'm not too choosy, but I'll admit breakfast is my favorite meal."

"Really?"

"Yes, really," he said firmly. "Are you going to quit dawdling so we can get to the cafeteria before they're all gone? They go fast."

"I doubt if they'll run out." She smiled at his

impatience but picked up her stride because Joe was already several steps ahead of her. Good thing, too, because Joe got the last two.

"Maybe they'll make more," she offered.

"Maybe," he answered hopefully. "Told you they were a hot item."

"Who would have thought?" she said wryly as she selected scrambled eggs, two slices of bacon and a small bowl of sliced fresh fruit. "I feel guilty for eating breakfast while everyone else is missing theirs."

"If we hadn't come down here, what would we have done?" he asked in a pragmatic tone. "Bought a stale donut from a machine and ate it in the staff lounge?"

"Probably."

"And which is healthier for us?"

She watched him drench his waffles in maple syrup. "Do you really want me to answer that?"

"No." His boyish grin made her heart do funny things in her chest. From the admiring looks he was getting from several nurses nearby, she wasn't the only one affected by his smile. At the same time, she wanted to preen under their gazes because *she* was the one who had his undivided attention. Better yet, *she* was more than a breakfast companion. She was his partner as well as the woman he trusted with his daughter.

However, it would be wise for her to remember that she was only the woman of the hour *for now*. Arthur had taught her that a mother figure could be easily replaced and he didn't have a fraction of the appeal that Joe Donatelli, fireman and paramedic, had.

"What are you going to do for the next two days?" he asked as he seemingly inhaled his meal.

"Today I'm going with a friend to shop for her wedding dress," she said.

"Where?" As Maggie narrowed her eyes speculatively, he added, "In case I need to reach you."

Just as she'd thought. He was scared to death of spending time alone with Breanna. "We're going to Kansas City."

"What time will you be home?"

His seemingly innocent tone didn't fool her. "Does it matter?"

His olive complexion darkened. "I thought you might like to come over for dinner tonight."

She was still having trouble reconciling this new cooperative and congenial Joe Donatelli with the old one, although admittedly she liked this version much better. "Dinner?"

"Yeah. I could throw a few burgers on the grill."

"Sounds great, but I'd better not promise anything," she said. "My friend, Trista, has vowed we're not coming home until she finds *The* Dress. How about tomorrow?"

"You don't have plans?"

"Other than working in my flower-beds, no. In fact, Breanna might like to dig in the dirt and I can always use someone who's handy with a shovel."

"Fair enough. We'll drive over first thing. You know what they say, 'The early bird gets the worm.'"

Somehow, she suspected he was already dreading the next twenty-four hours. She was also woman enough to be delighted by his eagerness to spend time with her, even if Breanna was the only reason for it.

"This bird isn't interested in worms," she said lightly. "Ten o'clock should be early enough for all of us."

Joe braced himself for the day ahead, but in spite of his pep talk that he could handle whatever happened with Breanna, a familiar knot of tension formed between his shoulder blades as soon as Nancy left the house. Resigned to the feeling for the foreseeable future and remembering Maggie's comment about how Breanna reacted to his anxiety, he tried to relax.

"OK, little Bee," he told the little girl as he sat at the table to feed her breakfast. "It's just you and me today, so let's try to make it go smoothly."

Breanna jiggled her ring of plastic keys and laughed at the noise she'd made before she opened her mouth like a baby bird for a spoonful of oatmeal.

She was happy—a good sign—and he was hopeful of success.

"So what should we do today?" he asked her. "Another trip to the park? Television? Or does a sandbox of your very own sound like fun? Nancy said you really liked playing in the one at the park yesterday."

The little girl smacked her lips and grunted in reply.

"OK, we'll see what we can find."

But when faced with his choices at the toy store, he wished Maggie had been there to give him advice. Should he buy molded plastic or build one out of lumber? If he went the do-it-yourself route, who would look after little Bee while he worked? And if he purchased one, which was better? One with a cover, or one without? The green turtle, blue fish or pink butterfly?

He wanted to call her on her cellphone and ask, as much to hear the sound of her voice as to hear her opinion, but he didn't want to abuse the privilege. In the end, out of sheer desperation because Breanna was now tired of the shopping excursion, he bought the turtle because she had toddled over to it and crawled inside.

As the day wore on, he found himself wishing Maggie was there to share in his successes—when Breanna played happily in her new sandbox—as well as his failures—when he couldn't convince the baby that a nap was the solution for being tired and cranky.

More importantly, he wanted Maggie at his side for more than the purpose of babysitting.

He wanted her there for himself.

He wanted to see the smile on her face and to hear her quiet voice and musical laugh. He wanted to observe her natural grace and appreciate it in ways he couldn't when they were on duty.

Most of all, he wanted to kiss her again.

Maggie had looked forward to The Great Wedding Dress Hunt for weeks, ever since Trista had gotten engaged. Yet, strangely enough, now that she was actually looking at gowns designed to put a woman in the middle of her own fairy-tale, she wanted to be elsewhere.

With Joe.

She tried to focus on lace and tulle, but his disappointed expression haunted her. She refused to feel guilty for having made plans—these had been made long before Breanna had come into his life—but she still felt as if she were letting Joe down by not being readily available. More than once, she caught herself checking her phone for missed calls. At times she caught herself wanting to phone him for an update, but she always held herself in check. After all, if Joe needed her, he'd contact her, wouldn't he?

But as the morning wore on and her phone remained uncannily silent, she was torn between wanting him to need her and relief that he obviously didn't. That would be a good thing, she told herself, because then their relationship could return to strictly professional boundaries.

Yet, deep down, she wasn't as happy at the notion of returning to those boundaries as she should be. As crazy as it was, as unwise as it was considering his single-parent status, she simply *liked* being in his company.

Perhaps she should have been worried about Breanna, but she wasn't. During the short time she'd seen Joe with the little girl, he'd watched over her with the same ferocity as a Templar knight guarding the Holy Grail. No, Breanna was in good hands.

Joe, however, was the one who worried her. She didn't want his day to be such a traumatic experience that he gave up on his promise to Dee before he gave himself a proper chance to learn his new role.

He might claim he wasn't father material, but her instincts said otherwise. For reasons he had yet to divulge, he'd simply convinced himself that he didn't have a paternal bone in his body.

Finally, she couldn't stand the unknown. After lunch at her favorite seafood restaurant, Maggie punched in Joe's number, trying not to give any special meaning to its place on her speed dial list.

"Donatelli."

"It's Maggie," she said softly, hoping he normally answered his cellphone in such a crisp manner rather than because he'd endured a difficult morning. "How's it going?"

"No bumps, bruises or blood, if that's what you're asking," he said gruffly.

She smiled at what was fast becoming his standard refrain. "Any problems?"

Silence greeted her and she pictured him raking his hair with his hand as he did when he was frustrated, which lately seemed to occur on a regular basis. "I guess not."

A howl in the background made her wince. "What's wrong?"

She heard his sigh. "She's tired and cranky. How's the shopping?"

He sounded impatient and she smiled. "Too many choices and all of them are beautiful." A crash, followed by another howl, reverberated in her ear.

"What happened?"

His voice was weary. "She just threw her blocks against the wall."

"Temper tantrum," she advised wisely. "She's mad about something."

"You think?" His sarcasm passed through the air waves loud and clear. "I'd love to chat, but I gotta go before she destroys the place."

"Do you want me to come home?" she asked.

He paused, as if debating with himself. "No," he finally said. "We'll manage."

"Maybe you could—" Before she finished her sentence with "put her to bed for a nap", he'd disconnected.

Ignorance really was bliss, she decided as she snapped her own phone closed. If she hadn't phoned, she could have spent the afternoon imagining the two of them having an uneventful time together. Now that she knew it wasn't the case, she wanted more than ever to be there.

For the next two hours she patiently endured flipping through what seemed like miles and miles of dress racks. Finally, Trista gazed at her sympathetically.

"Your heart isn't in this anymore, is it?" she asked.

"I'm sorry," Maggie apologized, "but no."

"It's Joe, isn't it?" The speculation on Trista's face suggested that her friend had seen through Maggie's forced enthusiasm for the last few hours. Her perception wasn't surprising—Trista had supported her through some tough times and had patiently listened to the story of Joe and Breanna as well as Maggie's own fears.

She nodded. "I think he's having a rough day and won't admit it."

"And you want to check on him."

"Yeah," she confessed. "I do."

"Look, Maggie…" Trista began.

Maggie held up her hands. "I know what you're going to say. I shouldn't have gotten involved with him and his daughter, but I can handle it."

"Did I say you couldn't?"

"No, but it's what you're thinking."

Trista's green-eyed gaze grew intent. "Yours is the only opinion that counts. And as long as you know to be careful, what else can I say except to ask what you are waiting for."

In spite of her friend's blessing, Maggie hesitated. "He said he'd manage on his own. He may not appreciate me dropping in unannounced."

"But you still want to see for yourself, don't you?"

Maggie sighed. "Yeah, it's crazy, isn't it?"

"I wouldn't call it *crazy*—" Trista said, but before she could finish, Maggie interrupted.

"Besides, today is all about you," she said firmly. "No one should shop for her wedding dress alone."

"Then it's a good thing I've seen all the dresses I want to see," Trista said lightly. "My feet hurt, and to be honest, they're all starting to look alike."

"But we still have a few more stores on your list," Maggie protested.

"So?" Trista said pragmatically. "We both like those three gowns I found in the first store the best. I say we pay that place another visit."

Maggie studied her friend for any signs of reluctance and found none. "You're certain. Absolutely, without a doubt certain this is what you want?"

"Positively. Now, let's wrap up this day so you can check on your hunky new partner."

"You're a star," Maggie said, hugging her impulsively.

Trista giggled. "I know, but it's always nice to hear it from my friends."

It took nearly an hour for Trista to choose the dress of her dreams, another hour to return to Trista's house where they had met early that morning, and an additional twenty minutes for Maggie to reach Joe's place. The traffic wasn't particularly heavy so Maggie used the time to devise a game plan. She didn't want to intrude or imply that she didn't think he couldn't handle Breanna, so she'd simply stop, say hello and reassure herself that he was indeed "managing", then be on her way. She'd be there five or ten minutes. Fifteen minutes, tops.

She parked on the driveway shortly before five o'clock and strolled up the walk, determined to stick to her time schedule. Because she didn't want to risk waking Breanna in case the little girl was napping, she bypassed the doorbell to knock softly on the frame.

When Joe didn't answer, she considered going home, but a mixture of concern and curiosity drove her to investigate. Thankful that Joe had shown her the flower-pot where he'd hidden his spare key for emergencies, she went around to the back and let herself inside.

In spite of the mess she encountered, total silence gave the house a deserted air. Dirty breakfast and dinner dishes rested on the counter and filled the sink. Wadded-up paper towels lay on the table as if there'd been a spill at some point. The tray of Breanna's highchair was still smeared with peas and bits of carrot.

The living room wasn't much better. Toys lay scattered across the floor. The morning newspaper was ripped to shreds and pieces of it had been flung everywhere. A half-full mug of cold coffee rested on the end table next to the recliner.

She'd expected to find the house with a well-lived-in look, but she certainly hadn't anticipated the sight of Joe sprawled in the recliner with Breanna tucked under his arm, covered with a fleece lap quilt.

Her heart twisted into a painful knot. If only she had a camera… Seeing him hold the little girl in a protective embrace, especially while he slept, couldn't have been more convincing evidence that he had more fathering instincts than he credited to himself.

In that instant she knew she was seeing a side of Joe Donatelli that he kept hidden, the side that he denied he possessed. This was the Joe Donatelli that Dee had known, the one Maggie's instincts had recognized. This was the Joe Donatelli who needed her to give him the confidence he so plainly lacked.

Dee, she was certain, would have wanted that.

Neither of them looked comfortable so, taking a chance, Maggie lifted Breanna out of his embrace. She grumbled, apparently protesting the loss of her human mattress, but didn't fully awaken. Joe didn't stir either, so she carried the little girl to her crib, covered her with her baby-sized comforter, then retraced her steps.

Joe hadn't budged an inch. Neither did he notice when she covered him with the same throw he'd used earlier. Clearly, he was exhausted, and after the busy shift they'd had at the station, he needed this nap as much as Breanna did.

Reassured, she decided it was time to slip out as quietly as she'd entered. Before she'd taken two steps, Joe shifted position, then suddenly bolted upright.

"Breanna?" he asked, his voice rusty.

"She's in her crib," she answered softly.

His tension visibly eased as he sank back into the recliner, looking dangerously handsome with his hair spiked in disarray and a dark shadow on his face. "For a second there I thought I'd dropped her."

"You didn't. I thought you'd both be more comfortable if she was in her own bed, so I moved her there."

"Thanks." Then, apparently gaining more of his wits, he stared at her in surprise. "Maggie?"

"In the flesh," she said cheerfully. "Trista found what she was looking for sooner than I'd expected—" she purposely glossed over the reason behind their decision "—so we decided to call it a day. I thought I'd check on you and when you didn't the answer the door, I used your spare key. I hope you don't mind."

His suddenly wide smile transformed his face. "No, I don't. In fact, I'm glad you did."

Under his appreciative gaze, a frisson of excitement skittered along her spine. "Then you missed me?" she teased.

"More than you know. I was counting the hours until tomorrow morning when I'd see you again."

Words to warm a woman's heart… "Rough day?" she commiserated.

A pained expression crossed his face. "We had our moments."

"You should have told me—" she began.

"I didn't want to call you away unless we had an emergency, so we muddled through. Fortunately, there were no bumps, bruises or…"

"Or blood," she finished.

"Exactly."

"So everything really went well? No crying sprees?"

"No major ones," he said. "She missed you, though."

For a woman who'd vowed to remain detached,

Joe's words brought her far more satisfaction than they should have. "Don't be silly," she said lightly. "She doesn't know me well enough."

"I think you'd be surprised."

After being on her feet all day, she perched on the sofa's edge. "We'll have to agree to disagree on that issue. What exactly did you two do to occupy yourselves?"

"Nancy said Breanna liked to play in the sandbox, so we went to the store and bought one. Then we spent the rest of the morning outside getting more sand in our clothes than we left in the box. After that came lunch. By the way, she hates peas."

Maggie grinned. "I guessed as much."

"She wanted to go out again after she ate, but it was nap time. I spent most of the afternoon trying to convince her that her droopy eyelids meant she was tired, but she wasn't buying it. Finally, I realized she wasn't paying attention to anything I said, so I let her do her own thing while I watched cable news."

"And once you did, she crawled into your lap."

He looked surprised. "How did you know? The minute she settled down, she was out. I couldn't risk waking her, so I caught forty winks of my own."

"You're definitely learning the tricks of the trade."

His disbelief was obvious in his glance. "What I want to know is why is she so docile for you and Nancy, but completely uncooperative when I'm in the picture?"

"She probably senses your own uneasiness and uncertainty and takes advantage of it. It'll get better, for both of you."

He didn't answer. He just stared at her, his gaze intent, his eyes filled with disbelief. "You're watching too many movies. Most situations don't have a happy ending."

"Sometimes we have to make our own."

"I suppose." He rubbed his eyes with a thumb and forefinger. "I wish I knew what Dee had been thinking."

"Do you still believe she made a mistake when she appointed you as Breanna's guardian?"

"Hell, yes, she made a mistake. A *huge* one. Even if Breanna is mine, which I sincerely doubt, Dee should have chosen someone else."

She chose to be practical. "She didn't, so you'll have to accept it and move on."

He pressed his mouth into a hard line. "I heard from my lawyer today. We're supposed to be at the lab at one o'clock tomorrow for the paternity test."

She'd hoped he had changed his mind, but he was clearly eager to find an escape clause from Dee's will. "You're certain you want to go this route?"

"I need to know the truth, Maggie. One way or another."

While situations were easier to accept when all questions had been answered, she was more afraid the knowledge could affect his relationship with his daughter for ever.

"Is it really that important?" she asked softly.

"It is to me."

"The truth is sometimes a mixed blessing," she said, speaking from her experience with Arthur. She'd been devastated when he'd announced he was leaving town so he could get back together with his childhood sweetheart. While she'd been planning their future, Arthur had been revisiting his past with his ex-girlfriend over the Internet.

"At times," he agreed, "but it's the only way I can make sense out of Dee's decision."

Somehow she suspected his vehemence was rooted in his own childhood, but his set jaw warned her not to press that sore spot.

"If you're that determined, I can't stop you, but I won't stand by and let Breanna suffer as a result."

"She won't. Now, can we talk about something else?"

They may as well, she thought, aggravated by his thick-headed maleness. On the other hand, she had another weapon in her arsenal... He obviously needed more moral support than she was providing. Perhaps if it came from another direction—from the station crew—he'd feel more optimistic and less inclined to break his promise.

Not that he would, but she didn't want to risk the possibility.

"By the way," she tacked on, "Captain Keller told me if there was anything you needed, to let him and the rest of the guys know. In fact, as an FYI, Shep's daughter is babysitter age, so if you ever want an evening free, I'm sure she'd be happy to watch Breanna."

"It's sad to think a fifteen-year-old kid can do a job that I can't," he muttered.

"Who said you can't? You've done well so far."

"Sheer luck."

"Don't be so hard on yourself. My brother felt

the same way you did when he brought his first child home. A week later, he was handling Sam like a pro."

He eyed her carefully. "What makes you certain I'll do the same? Some men simply aren't cut out to be fathers."

"You aren't one of them," she said simply. "You're a man who does what needs to be done, regardless of the situation—a man who's made rescuing people his life's work. I've only worked with you for a few weeks, but I know how you hate to fail at anything. As far as I'm concerned, Breanna couldn't have anyone better watching over her."

"Yet you called and stopped by to check on us."

"Only out of curiosity," she defended, unwilling to admit that she'd been too impatient to wait another day to see him again. "One partner looking out for the other."

Her face warmed with her half-truth and his gaze grew speculative, as if he could tell she wasn't being completely honest—that in spite of their careers being a temporary stumbling block, she wanted an opportunity to kiss him again.

"Is that all it is?" he asked.

"No," she grumbled. "As crazy as it sounds, I

just wanted to see you." Because she didn't want his head to swell, she added, "And Breanna."

He answered with a lazy grin. "Really?"

"Yes, really," she said sharply, hating it that he'd forced her to admit what she was still trying to understand herself. Coming here had definitely been a bad idea, she decided before she rose. "As it's plain you have everything under control, I'll leave you two—"

"Wait." He lowered the footrest and stood. "Don't go. Stay for dinner."

"I shouldn't."

"Why not? It won't be fancy—I'll grill a few burgers—but I hate eating alone."

He looked so hopeful that she hated to disappoint him. And for what? To go home to an empty house where she'd spend the rest of the evening wondering what he was doing? Her plan may have allowed a fifteen-minute visit, but what would another hour matter? Besides, she *was* hungry and she wasn't fond of dining alone either…

"A hamburger sounds perfect. While you're fixing dinner, I'll wake Breanna."

He visibly winced. "Do you have to?"

"If she sleeps too long now, she won't sleep tonight," she warned.

He shuddered. "In that case, wake her."

"I thought you'd see things my way."

"One thing, though," he said before she headed down the hallway, "if she isn't happy about having her nap cut short, make sure she knows it was your idea and not mine. I'm already operating at a disadvantage and I don't need any more points against me."

Maggie laughed at his droll tone. "Your wish is my command."

If only that were true. Joe gazed appreciatively at the sight Maggie presented as she walked away. If he'd thought she looked great in jeans, she was positively breathtaking in her knee-length khaki skirt. Her shapely legs with those miles of soft, tanned skin were more than his extremely vivid imagination had conjured up. The urge to tiptoe after her and haul her into his bedroom grew strong, especially when his mental picture included seeing her stretched across his sheets with her lips parted invitingly.

Dammit! He shouldn't be thinking along those lines. She was his *partner,* for heaven's sake, not one of the groupies who hung around the sports bar where he and the rest of the guys went on the weekends! Unfortunately, in spite of his mental scolding, in spite of her being his professional "other half", he still wanted her in the worst way.

And between Maggie's honesty and his suspicions, the feeling was mutual.

He was sweating before he went outside to stand in the late afternoon sun to tend the barbecue grill. As he struck the match, he realized his attraction to Maggie had sparked and grown to the flaming stage just as quickly as the wooden stick in his hand.

He hadn't been celibate over the years, but he certainly wasn't the Casanova the guys at the station thought he was. He was too picky to be indiscriminate when it came to female companionship. Normally, though, he sought out women who were experienced at the flirtation and seduction game when he needed to scratch that particular itch, but in spite of his selectivity he couldn't remember a single one by name or face since he'd met Maggie.

She simply outshone them all.

Her smile was genuine; her laugh came easily. She didn't try to impress him with her words or her actions; everything she said was sincere and open and honest and her actions were an extension of her principles. She possessed a lively mind, was quick to defend those she considered weaker and wasn't afraid to disagree or challenge him.

If he looked hard enough, he could find similarities between her and Dee, but as comfortable as he'd been with Deanna, Maggie simply made him feel *alive.*

Which was why seeing Maggie when he'd woken up had been as exhilarating as receiving an unexpected check in the mail. Just as extra funds gave one a bit of financial breathing room, Maggie's unplanned arrival did the same. Granted, his day hadn't been all bad, but something had been missing.

It had been Maggie, which was why he'd alternated between counting down the hours until tomorrow and reaching for the phone.

Now, with her here, life was suddenly good—not because he would relinquish his parenting duties but because of the way she made him feel.

His simple meal of burgers and oven-baked french fried potatoes came and went, but he deftly maneuvered her into staying longer.

"You have to watch little Bee playing in her sandbox," he coaxed. "She's mesmerized when sand gets between her toes."

Maggie's laughter reminded him of wind

chimes swaying in a light breeze. "Admit it. You just want me to be the one to drag her out of there when it's time for a bath."

He pretended affront. "Who, me? Would I do such a thing?"

She laughed. "Yes, you would."

"OK, guilty as charged, but if you stay, I solemnly promise I won't ask you to be the bad guy."

"I appreciate your consideration," she said wryly, "but I really should go home."

Joe hated to see her leave. "What could be better than sitting outside on a nice night like tonight, listening to the birds chirp and watching the sun set?"

"I've been gone all day. I have laundry waiting, a house to clean…"

"All of which will still be there tomorrow," he coaxed. "How does the saying go? 'Housework is never done'?"

She bit on her lower lip in obvious indecision.

"Come on," he wheedled. "What's more important than spending time with a friend?"

Slowly, she nodded, her smile weak. "What indeed?"

CHAPTER SIX

JOE DONATELLI was like pure milk chocolate, Maggie thought as she puttered around her kitchen the next morning, preparing for the moment when he arrived. She'd always been careful to limit herself to one small piece when the craving struck, but too much of it ruined her waistline. Likewise, too much of Joe wasn't a good thing.

She was simply too weak to resist temptation.

While she knew the dangers and understood the risks of over-indulgence, she simply hadn't been able to tear herself away after dinner last night to go home where she belonged.

As it had turned out, she'd stayed long enough to wash the dishes while Joe had put Breanna to bed. When a sense of déjà vu struck her, she dismissed it.

The situation with Joe was different, she'd told

herself. It had a beginning and an established end. There wouldn't be any surprises or unexpected developments because no promises had been made or implied and there were certainly no expectations of either. In a few weeks Joe should be more than capable of handling his daughter on his own and she would walk away, her heart and soul intact. The only emotion she'd feel would be satisfaction for a job well done.

Yes, she'd mapped everything out; the situation was under control. With that control came the freedom to sit back and savor each moment with Joe and his daughter while she built a store of fond memories.

As she glanced out the window, her heart skipped with anticipation as she saw the man occupying her thoughts strolling up the walk with a diaper bag slung over one arm and a little girl perched on the other.

She greeted them just as Joe had bent down far enough for Breanna to lean out and press the doorbell. "Hi, you two. Are you ready for a fun day?"

Breanna leaned forward, her arms outstretched as she jabbered away. Maggie took her, then addressed Joe. "I hope you remembered to bring a change of clothes for Breanna, otherwise she'll be a fright when you take her to your appointment."

His shoulders slumped and he slapped his forehead. "Aw. I didn't. I only remembered extra diapers and bottles of formula."

Sensing Joe's disgust with himself and afraid he'd see it as another inadequacy in a long string of inadequacies, she tried to minimize the damage. "Diapers and formula are good. As for her clothes, we'll save the dirt-digging for later, after your trip to the hospital."

"I can run home," he began.

"Not necessary," she assured him. "I was going to buy a new ceiling fan for my bedroom this afternoon but we'll do it now. The one I have makes a horrible racket and my dad's coming over this weekend to replace it."

"I can do that for you," he offered. "I may not be a licensed electrician, but I can install a ceiling fan. After playing Mr. Mom, I'm ready to take on something I can handle with my eyes closed."

Her eyes lit up. "Great. As much as I love my dad and appreciate everything he does, he isn't the handiest man to have around the house. I usually end up calling in someone else to finish the job he started," she said ruefully.

Joe smiled, grateful not only for the opportunity to repay Maggie a favor but also to tackle a project for which he was suited. After completely missing the mark when he hadn't thought to bring a spare set of clothes for Breanna, this handyman chore couldn't have come at a better time. "Then what are we waiting for? We'll call in at my place on the way so I can pick up my toolbox."

An hour later, with toolkit in hand and the new ceiling fan unboxed, he flicked the wall switch in Maggie's bedroom. The blades began to turn and as Maggie had warned, the motor made the most horrible grinding noise he'd heard in a long time. "Ouch."

She laughed as she held Breanna on one hip. "I told you it sounded awful."

"And you were right." He looked at Breanna. "Wasn't she right, squirt?"

The little girl giggled and held out her arms.

"Sorry, kiddo, but you'll have to wait until I fix this for Maggie." So, with the two of them looking on, he began to work.

As he unwound screws and attached wires, his sense of worth slowly returned. Mechanical things were so much easier to deal with than a little person. Everything worked according to a

set series of laws that were really quite simple—
no power, no operation. If he made a mistake, he
could undo it and start again.

Children, on the other hand, didn't come with
instructions and they didn't operate in the same
logical and orderly manner as equipment did.
More importantly, there weren't opportunities
for do-overs.

The responsibility was overwhelming, as was
the temptation to renege on the bargain he'd
made with Dee and with Maggie. Yet, he couldn't
go back on his word. Not yet, anyway.

Twenty minutes later, he was gently trying to
convince Breanna to swap a kitchen spatula for
the screwdriver she'd commandeered out of his
kit. Instead of handing over his tool, she smiled
and giggled as if she thought they were playing
a game. He suddenly realized how far the little
girl had come since the morning he'd first
brought her home when she'd clung to her bunny
with both arms and hardly made a sound as she
stared wide-eyed at her new surroundings.

Today, however, she'd left Mr. Bugs on
Maggie's bed and was exploring everything from
the contents of the closet to what lay behind the
dust ruffle. She'd also checked out Joe's toolbox,

banged his wrenches like they were drumsticks instead of expensive tools, and emptied most of his screwdrivers and other assorted items onto the carpeted floor as if they were her toys, too.

He couldn't credit Breanna's adjustment only to the passage of time. In his opinion, the major factor was Maggie herself. Her ready smile, her soothing voice, her gentle touch had been just what the little girl—and he—had needed.

He realized something else, too.

Whenever he'd helped his various foster-parents with their projects, he'd always felt as if he were somehow intruding, as if he were there on sufferance, an outsider looking in. Today, however, with Maggie and little Bee in this family setting, he had a taste of belonging, as if he were part of something bigger than himself.

He likened the feeling to the camaraderie and the close-knit bond he'd formed with the guys at the fire station, but this seemed far more personal, far more intimate. Whatever it was, though, he wanted it to last. He simply had to convince Maggie to stick around longer than their agreed-on month. Considering how she seemed to dote on the little girl, maybe it wouldn't be too difficult. In fact, she had probably become far more emotionally involved than she'd intended to.

"All done," he said cheerfully, as he picked up Breanna to stand under the silently running fan and watched her wide-eyed delight at the breeze ruffling her hair.

The smile on Maggie's face was equally dazzling. "Thanks, Joe. I can't thank you enough." She stood on tiptoe and brushed a kiss against his cheek.

Joe recognized opportunities when he saw them and this was opportunity with a capital O. He instantly snaked his free arm around her waist and pulled her close. Her breathless "Oh" disappeared against his mouth as he deepened his kiss and he savored her softness, her honeyed fragrance and her taste.

Falling under her spell, his grip tightened until she was plastered against him. Her lips parted to allow him in and he didn't hesitate. The urge to crawl inside her skin grew strong and the thin layer of clothing between them seemed like too much of a barrier.

His hand splayed across her back and his fingers meandered up and down her spine, causing her to quiver as she leaned into him. Her open palm rested on his biceps with a touch that seemed to burn into his muscle. Oh, how he wanted her fingers, her mouth and her gorgeous body all over his, and then he wanted to reciprocate, taking hours and hours to explore every delectable inch of her.

Breanna suddenly squirmed and protested, effectively dousing his lustful flames but not completely eliminating the embers. As he pulled away to notice Maggie's dazed expression, satisfaction filled his soul. "For a payback like that," he said, flashing her a lazy grin, "any other handyman projects I can do for you?"

Her face turned pink as she put a half-step's worth of space between them. "None I can think of at the moment."

"A pity." He pretended a sigh. "If you do, let me know."

"You don't mind? Handling repairs, that is?"

He was certain his grin had turned feral because if there was one thing he didn't mind, it was kissing her until her toes curled. Whatever task she found would be worth the reward. "For you? Not at all."

Breanna cupped his face in her tiny hands, turned his chin in her direction, then bussed his cheek before she cocked her head as if to study his response.

"Do you want some of this action too, little missy?" he teased, and blew a strawberry against her neck.

Breanna chortled and wiggled in his arms. "More," she demanded, and he complied.

"You've made remarkable progress with her," Maggie commented.

"Progress? Maybe. Remarkable? Hardly. I feel more like the horse still standing at the starting gate while the others are halfway around the track," he confessed.

"Compared to the first day I saw you together, you've both come a long way. If I was going to guess, I'd say that holding her while she napped made a difference. Sleeping with a guy changes a girl's perspective, you know." She grinned.

His imagination took off as he thought about how he'd like to test that theory with Maggie. "It may have changed Breanna's, but I prefer my bed partners to be a lot older. About twenty-seven years older."

"I'm gratified to hear that," she said wryly, her faint blush suggesting that she'd connected the dots he'd supplied, "but the point is, she's starting to trust you."

"Let's hope so." If he accomplished nothing else, he intended to accomplish that. He didn't want Breanna to lose her faith in people like he had, because it was nearly impossible to regain.

At that moment Breanna twisted herself out of Joe's hold and dove toward Maggie before he could stop her. A painful heartbeat later he relaxed as Maggie laughingly caught and hugged her before smooching her forehead.

He'd seen spontaneous acts like this before between his foster-mothers and their children and the sight had always been bittersweet. He may never have experienced them for himself, but even as a kid he'd known what had prompted them.

Love.

Oddly enough, he was jealous of his own daughter.

"I'd say she trusts someone else, too," he said casually.

Maggie gave in to Breanna's demand and set her on the floor, where she toddled back to Joe's toolbox. "Perhaps to some degree," she said, straightening, "but you're the constant in her life. I'm not."

"You're around her almost as much as I am."

She grew thoughtful. "Maybe, but she shouldn't learn to depend on me."

"Why not?"

"Because our agreement only covered a short period of time in which I would help you learn how to be a father. After that, I won't be in her life."

That wasn't what he wanted to hear. "Ever?"

"Maybe not *ever,* but definitely not on a regular basis."

"I disagree," he said. "In fact, I predict you won't be able to stay away."

She raised a sculpted eyebrow. "Oh?"

"You won't, because you love her."

Until he'd said those words aloud, he hadn't realized the difficult position in which he'd placed Maggie. He'd seen her affection for the little girl, but he hadn't understood the strength or the depth of those feelings until today. In spite of the possibility that he might relinquish his guardianship, that she might lose Breanna as she'd lost Zach and Tyler, she'd still fallen in love with the little girl.

That was the difference between them. He insulated himself to avoid getting hurt because he expected the worst. Maggie, on the other hand, waded in and gave all of herself in spite of an uncertain outcome, because she hoped for the best. Suddenly he felt guilty for putting her in this potentially ill-fated position because he'd never wanted to hurt her.

Her expression froze for an instant. "Don't be ridiculous, Joe."

He didn't let her dismissive tone or her denial stop him; he pressed on because he knew he was right. "If you didn't, you wouldn't have dropped by yesterday to check on us and you wouldn't have spent the whole day worrying about how we were doing."

"OK," she groused, "I dropped by because I was worried, but worry doesn't imply any special affection."

"Says you."

"Says me," she insisted. "I'd hoped everything would run smoothly and was afraid it wouldn't. And if it didn't…"

He fell silent, waiting for her to continue.

"You said you'd re-evaluate the situation when your test results arrived," she said. "I didn't— *don't*—want you to give up before then."

Pretending her feelings didn't exist was clearly her defense mechanism to avoid suffering through the same pain as in her previous relationship. He knew because he recognized the strategy and used it himself. However, he was surprised and a little hurt that she doubted his character. "You really thought I'd break my promise?"

"No!" Her emphatic answer raised his spirits somewhat. "I just didn't want you to be tempted. The mind can play tricks when a person is exhausted and his guard is down. Who knows what you might have talked yourself into?"

"You got that right," he mumbled to himself before he spoke in a normal tone. "Then it would bother you if I decided to pass on being a father?" He raised an eyebrow.

"Of course it would. Breanna needs you." Impatience laced her tone. "Besides, the Joe Donatelli I know doesn't run from tough situations. The question is, do you know the same guy?"

"I met him a time or two," he answered ruefully, "but I'll be honest. The thought had crossed my mind several times." As far as he was concerned, his childhood experiences didn't make him the best man for the job, even if Breanna *was* his daughter—a fact that still remained to be seen.

"And?" she demanded.

"I won't give up because I have a rough day or a sleepless night," he vowed. "The next few weeks are for me to learn if I have what it takes to be the father she needs, provided I *am* her father, but after encountering sad situations in our line of work, you know as well as I that biology isn't a guarantee of being a good parent. Which is why I'm counting on you to stick by us, for as long as we need you."

"We agreed on—"

"For as long as we need you," he repeated. "If the results say she's mine, I want my safety net to be available for more than thirty days." He left unsaid what would happen if the report said otherwise—he'd deal with the moral dilemma of his promise to Dee later.

She bit her lip, then nodded. "All right, but no sudden decisions, no surprises. I don't want to wake up one day and discover everything's changed because you made a spur-of-the-moment decision."

He was puzzled. "Like what?"

"You could relocate. Find a girlfriend. Any number of things."

"I won't make a move without discussing it

with you first." He hadn't realized how important this one detail meant to her until he saw her eyes brighten with unspeakable relief.

"Thanks, Joe. I…" Her voice broke and she paused for a second. "Thanks."

As she fled the room, Joe smiled. For the first time since Breanna had come into his life he felt as if he'd finally done something right.

You love her. Joe's statement echoed in Maggie's mind throughout dinner, during Breanna's bath, while the little girl demanded her bedtime story and hugged her good-night.

Maggie simply didn't want to admit his comment was true—she'd fought so hard against becoming attached. It *couldn't* be true, she told herself. She was fond of the toddler, just as she was fond of her nieces and nephews. Her feelings didn't go any deeper than that.

It wasn't until she went home to her quiet house that she reluctantly admitted Joe was right. She *did* love the little girl.

She had an equally tough time admitting that she was falling in love with Joe. She didn't want to develop deeper feelings for him but the more time they spent together, the more difficult it became to think of him as just a friend and colleague who needed her help.

Perhaps if he wasn't trying so hard to do the right thing. Perhaps if he would act more self*ish*ly instead of self*less*ly. Perhaps if he just threw up his hands, gave up and walked away. But he didn't take any of those paths. And because he didn't, he'd gained her respect, her admiration, and what she feared was love.

She couldn't love him; wouldn't even consider it because, given the potential for heartache, it wouldn't be one of the smarter things she could do. Severing personal ties with her partner, whether it happened on her terms or on his, would be far more devastating than when she'd lost Arthur because if she was honest, his two boys had captured more of her heart than their father had. Her feelings for Joe, whether it was love or its precursor, had already grown deeper and more intense than the combined emotions she'd felt for Arthur and his children.

Even so, she wouldn't fool herself into thinking that Joe reciprocated her sentiments. Oh, sure, they didn't have any trouble striking enough sparks off each other to start a forest fire, but she'd mistaken "appreciation" for love before. She wouldn't do it again, no matter how quickly his lazy grin made her feel as if she were tumbling head first off a cliff.

And if she couldn't wait for morning to arrive so she could drive to the station, it was only because she loved her job. Her excitement had nothing to do with the prospect of seeing Joe again…

"Donatelli. Randall." Harry barked their names as he approached while they were running through their usual ambulance check after they reported for duty. "Are you two ready for your Boy Scouts tonight?"

Maggie groaned inwardly at his reminder. "We will be," she said instead.

"They'll be here at seven."

As soon as he moved away, Joe eyed her. "Boy Scouts?"

"Yeah. I forgot all about them. When I worked the other day, a troop leader called and asked the captain if someone could give an hour-long session on basic first aid. I told him we would, but I got caught up in other things and forgot about it."

"How old are the boys?"

"I assume twelve and older."

His mouth twisted into a wry grin. "You haven't dealt with Scouts before, have you?"

"I've shown elementary school kids the ambulance. Does that count?" she asked hopefully.

He shook his head. "Not unless they only want a tour. If they're asking us to teach them enough first aid so they earn their merit badges, it's a whole new situation."

"Merit badges? Sounds involved."

"It is."

"Then you have experience."

"I've helped a few boys with the requirements," he admitted, "but covering all the material takes several sessions. Unless they're only looking for a tour, one night won't be nearly enough. We should find out what their, goals and expectations are before they land on our doorstep."

"As I'm clearly the novice, I'll bow to your judgment. Just tell me what to do and when."

By six forty-five that evening, Maggie was amazed by Joe's preparations. He'd discovered the boys' leader, who normally taught the first aid segment, had recently undergone a triple bypass operation, which meant the boys needed someone to fill in the gap.

Joe, however, was undaunted by the task or its

short notice. He downloaded the most recent information from the official Boy Scout Web site and proceeded to outline the coursework over the next several weeks, assigning certain topics to Maggie to cover.

The six boys arrived on time, all wearing their uniforms with pride and appearing both awed and eager to learn first aid from the "pros", as one teen called them. After watching Joe with Breanna, Maggie couldn't wait to see how he interacted with adolescents.

He did fine. Better than fine. He did great. He welcomed them, spoke to them as if their opinions mattered, and in general treated them with respect.

In turn, she watched the boys' reactions to Joe's lecture. None seemed to daydream or fidget, indicating that his unique mix of humor and earnestness had captured their attention.

"Who knows what the word *triage* means?" he asked.

A studious-looking, tall, sandy-haired boy raised his hand. "It has to do with sorting people for treatment so those who are hurt the worst are taken care of first."

"Excellent. How many of you have heard of standard precautions?"

The same youth's hand shot up. "It's when you treat everyone's blood as if it's infected with something like HIV or hepatitis."

"Very good."

"Drew knows that 'cause his dad's a doctor," another boy volunteered.

"Now you know what those words mean, too," Joe answered.

As he led them into a discussion on blood-borne pathogens, Maggie saw how confidently Joe handled himself. Clearly, he was in his element, as if being a paramedic gave him an identity and a sense of purpose. She simply had to figure out a way to convince him that being Breanna's father, regardless of her paternity, could be equally fulfilling, if not more so.

"Who has a first-aid kit in their house?" Joe asked.

Only Drew's hand shot up. The other boys groaned good-naturedly.

"For those of you who don't have an emergency kit, what do you think should be stocked in it?"

"Band-Aids."

"Cotton balls."

"Alcohol." As all eyes turned onto the youth who'd supplied this answer, his fair skin turned bright red under his blond hair. "Not the stuff you drink," he defended. "The stuff they use in the doctor's office before you get a shot."

"Rubbing alcohol," Joe explained. "Excellent. But did you know, in the old days they used whiskey for disinfecting purposes?"

"I thought they just gave that to the guys to get 'em so drunk they didn't know they were hurting," another answered.

"That was only when they were doing surgery," a third boy said knowledgeably. "Then they gave 'em a bullet to bite on."

The discussion went downhill after that. Joe's eyes met Maggie's and she didn't hide her smile. "Way to go, partner," she mouthed. "Let's see you get out of this one."

His smile broad, Joe raised his hands to quieten the small group, but the voice over the loud-speaker did the job for him. "Squad two. Report of unidentified male with apparent seizure. Twelve fifteen Fairfield Drive."

Maggie immediately recognized the address as the location of a rundown hotel that rented rooms by the week or the hour, depending on the clientele. She grabbed their jackets off the hooks near the ambulance while Joe wrapped up his class.

"Your assignment is to assemble a first-aid kit using the list of supplies in your manual," he told the boys. "Bring them next week and we'll discuss their purposes. See you then."

The boys and their leader watched in wide-eyed interest as Joe and Maggie shrugged on their jackets, hopped into the ambulance, and headed down the concrete driveway with the required red lights and siren.

"You squeaked out of that one," Maggie teased as Joe drove towards their destination. "Who would have thought their minds would run in the direction of television medicine?"

"It's a guy thing. When you're that age, it's a lot more manly to think about biting on a bullet than depending on the chemistry of a puny injection."

"I'll take my painkiller any day."

"Me, too." He pointed toward the patrol car that signaled their destination. "We're here."

Inside, the bewhiskered hotel clerk who looked thirty years older than he probably was gave them directions. "Fourth floor. Third room on the left. No elevator."

"It figures," Joe mumbled under his breath. "We can't use our gurney."

"Could be worse."

His disgust was obvious. "I'm going back for a stretcher." He returned a few minutes later with the compact stretcher they used for tight-space situations.

"Ready?" Without waiting for his reply, she hefted a bag on one shoulder, expecting Joe to take the other, then headed for the stairwell. Joe, however, had other plans.

He shouldered her aside once they reached the fire door. "Stay behind me."

His imperious attitude irked her. "What did you say?"

"I'm going first." He pushed his way through and started up the first flight.

"Says who?" Irritated, she followed.

"Says me."

"It's my turn," she reminded him. "We had an agreement. You can't break it whenever the mood strikes you."

"Sue me." He wrinkled his nose in disgust. "What *is* that smell?"

A breath-taking aroma of rotting food and body waste grew stronger as they climbed onto the third floor landing. "I don't want to know, but, whatever it is, we're not opening that door unless we have to."

Joe glanced over his shoulder at her. "This is definitely worse than not having an elevator."

"To put it mildly," she agreed, grateful for the sturdy boots she wore. Who knew what she'd encounter in the dark corners of the stairwell? From the scurrying noises, she hoped it had only been mice and not rats.

On the fourth floor, outside their patient's room, Officer Derek Pruett stood sentry, then motioned them forward as soon as he noticed them. "In here."

She wasn't surprised Joe continued to lead the way. In any event, she wasn't going to complain about his highhandedness in public. She'd save that for when this was over. Meanwhile, she understood why Pruett remained in the hallway—the distinct smell of urine permeated the air, along with other breath-taking odors she didn't want to identify.

"What do we have?" Joe asked Pruett's partner, Officer Thomas Krom, who was crouched beside their patient.

"According to the clerk downstairs, Martin Kazinsky is in his mid-forties and never had seizures before. Apparently Kazinsky drops in when the weather's cold, stays a few days, then leaves."

"Is he alone? Who found him like this?"

"No one will admit to anything," Pruett supplied from his place at the doorway. "Probably because the guests at this fine establishment aren't the most law-abiding citizens in town."

"Respirations adequate," Maggie reported to Joe, breathing through her mouth to avoid the smell.

"Pulse is strong. Looks malnourished. Whiskey bottles in the corner. Alcoholic, I'd say."

Pruett stuck his head through the open doorway. "There's an altercation on the first floor we need to check out. Are you two OK by yourselves for a little while?"

"Sure. Go ahead," Joe said while Maggie nodded and bent as close to their patient's ear as her nose could tolerate.

"Mr Kazinsky," she asked. "Martin? We're paramedics from the fire department. Can you hear us? We need to talk to you."

Immediately, Martin's body spasmed. "Watch his airway," Joe instructed.

By the time his muscle contractions eased, nearly a minute had passed. And when they couldn't rouse him after the episode, Joe began assembling his IV equipment. "I'll start normal saline while you get him on O."

Maggie immediately affixed a non-rebreathing mask on Martin's face, which would deliver the highest concentration of oxygen. As she settled the mask to her satisfaction and pulled the elastic band over his skull, she noticed a raised area near the back of his head.

"Look at this." She pointed to the spot. "This isn't a marked knot, so it's hard to say if this is his normal skull shape or not." She flashed her penlight on his head. "It's definitely bruised."

"He either fell and hit his head when he had a seizure, or the seizure is a result of his fall," Joe answered. "The docs will have to sort that out."

Maggie wordlessly prepared the injections of thiamine and dextrose per their standing orders while Joe established his IV line. As soon as Joe began to administer the dextrose through the port, Martin stiffened again.

"He's going from one convulsion to the next. I'm going to give him some help," she told Joe, mentally defying him to disagree.

He didn't. "We don't have a choice."

Maggie reached into the drug kit and prepared another injection of a tranquilizer that contained both muscle-relaxant and anti-convulsant properties. As soon as Joe administered this dose, Martin's seizure ended, although he remained unresponsive.

"Let's get him out of here," Joe said.

A few minutes later they had rolled Martin onto a stretcher. While Joe called the dispatcher to learn the status of Pruett and Krom, Maggie strapped down Martin for the trip downstairs.

"They're still busy," Joe told her as he finished his radio conversation. "Who knows how long it will be, so we'll have to do this on our own."

"Naturally," she said wryly.

"I'd send you downstairs with our stuff, but it isn't a good idea to split up. Leaving our supplies and coming back for them later isn't an option either."

"I agree."

He eyed her. "Can you carry a bag while we…?"

As if she'd claim weakness. She didn't work out to stay in shape for nothing. "Try and stop me."

Maggie slung one of their first-responder bags around her neck while Joe took the other. As if on cue, three street toughs wearing leather and chains swaggered in.

"Well, lookee here, Mo." The one with purple and green hair studied Maggie with a wicked grin. "Ain't she sweet?"

Their cocky attitudes set off alarm bells in her head but these men were the sort who plainly thrived on instilling fear and she wasn't about to accommodate them. "Step aside," she ordered, ignoring his leer. "This man needs a doctor."

Before she took two steps toward her end of the stretcher, the second fellow, his hair closely cropped and sporting rings in his eyebrows and lower lip, moved close enough for her to smell his fetid breath. His red eyes and runny nose were characteristic of a cocaine user, which made him unpredictable at best. Wariness swept over her.

"Move along, guys," Joe commanded. "You're in our way."

"Well, whadya know, boys," Purple-hair sneered. "We're in their way."

Maggie didn't like the situation and the sooner they got downstairs to their ambulance, the better. "You heard us. Step aside so we can do our job."

"In good time, sister," the third fellow with tattoos all over his hands said lazily as he maneuvered himself between her and Joe. "In good time. What's up with grandpa here?"

"He's had a seizure," she said shortly, not liking the way the other two had surrounded Joe, effectively isolating her. A healthy dose of fear suddenly shot through her system.

"He owes us money," Ring-face said importantly.

"He'll have to pay up later."

Tattoo Hands stepped closer, wedging her against the wall. "We want our money now."

"Leave her alone," Joe demanded.

Maggie mentally signaled Joe to call for help on the radio, but out of the corner of her eye she saw he couldn't. Purple Hair and Ring-face had closed in and Joe clearly wanted to keep his hands free.

Tattoo Hands ran a finger down her cheek. It took everything she had not to shiver or show her fear. "Got any money, sister?"

"No, and I'm not your sister."

His twisted smile revealed blackened teeth. "Ain't that nice? But if you don't have any money, I'll bet you've got something better in your bags. Some pick-me-ups, if you know what I mean."

He wanted her drug box! She gripped the handle. "Sorry. You're out of luck."

"I don't think so." With lightning speed, he grabbed at her bag and she fought to hold on to it with both hands. A few well-placed kicks met their mark if Tattoo Hands' grunts were any indication. In the background, she heard Joe shout, followed by the unmistakable thud of fists hitting flesh. Just when she was certain she and Joe were doomed, Pruett and Krom raced in to join the scuffle.

Tattoo Hands shoved her hard enough to send her to the floor, where she landed painfully on one hip, before he scurried out of the room, empty-handed.

Joe crouched beside her, his face wreathed in worry as he began to run his hands down her legs and arms while she caught her breath. "Maggie? You OK?"

She took stock of her aches and pains. "Yeah. How about you?"

"A little sore, but nothing serious."

She finally heard the grunts of the would-be thieves as the two officers effectively restrained them on the floor, each with a patrolman's knee in the middle of his back and each spouting invectives she'd never heard before in spite of her years on the streets.

"I saved my bag."

His eyes flashed with fury. "Damn it, Maggie! You should have given it to them. They could have hurt you."

"I couldn't hand over our drug box. Can you imagine what they would have done with the medicine? They would have sold it on the street for a small fortune. They'd brag about what they did and the next thing you know, they and others like them would try the same stunt with other paramedics. I refuse to let them bully us."

"Not at the expense of your safety."

"It's over, Joe. Forget it. Now, help me up, will you?"

He reached out and pulled her to her feet. Immediately, her hip protested and she stumbled against him, grateful he'd been nearby to keep her from taking another tumble. For a long moment she simply leaned against him, happy for his rock-solid strength.

"Maybe you need to sit down?" he suggested.

"Where?" she asked wryly. "I'm fine. Give me a minute to walk it off and we'll go."

Pruett and Krom hauled their prisoners to their feet. "We can get rid of these two and come back and help you," Pruett said, "or if you can handle him…" he inclined his head toward the stretcher "…you can follow us down."

"We'll follow."

"We'll wait."

Their answers came simultaneously. "The patient comes first," Maggie reminded him. "We've wasted enough time. We'll follow at our own pace."

The truth was, Maggie's hip hurt and she could easily imagine the huge bruise that was forming. Neither the hip nor the bruise would improve over the next few minutes and she'd rather make their descent while her adrenaline high was strong enough for her to ignore the pain.

"Suit yourself," Pruett answered. "If you haven't made it down by the time we get these two taken care of, we'll be back."

"Fair enough."

Joe frowned. "You shouldn't be carrying anyone, much less an unconscious man, down four flights of stairs. What if you can't—?"

"I can do my job," she insisted. "It isn't as if Martin weighs three hundred pounds and I'm doing this alone. Calling for more help will take time he doesn't have."

Still he frowned, but Maggie ignored him. "If we go slowly, the two of us can handle him." At his obvious hesitation, she added, "I know my limitations, Joe. Trust me, I can do this."

He leveled a hard gaze at her. Slowly, reluctantly, he nodded as if her confidence had satisfied him to some degree. "OK. Ready on three?"

Carrying Martin as well as her bag was a strain, but it wasn't the first time she'd had to push herself—it went with the territory. Halfway between the second and third floors, Maggie's muscles burned from exertion. Sheer determination and pride demanded she keep going because if she stopped, she was afraid she wouldn't start again.

"Are you doing OK?" Joe asked over his shoulder.

"Yeah," she huffed, grateful he was leading and couldn't see her expression. But no sooner had she said so than the unexpected happened. Just as she was stepping onto the second-floor landing, something scurried underneath her foot and she lost her balance.

The stretcher wobbled as she shifted her weight in those few seconds to regain her footing. She couldn't drop their patient, she simply couldn't! In spite of feeling as if the whole episode progressed in slow motion, it only took a second. One second to marshal her strength to hold onto her end of the stretcher, one second to keep from pitching forward onto the grimy concrete floor.

One second to know that she couldn't do anything except minimize the damage.

She came down hard on her left knee. Pain shot through her leg and she squeezed her eyes closed to hold back the tears.

"Maggie." Joe's command gradually registered on her brain. "What happened? Are you all right? Answer me, Maggie."

She cleared her throat and swallowed the nausea. "A mouse or something tripped me. I'm OK. Just a little...I'm OK," she repeated.

"I'm setting down my end," he told her. "Don't move until I get there."

"No," she said through teeth gritted against the ache. "We have to get our patient downstairs ASAP. I'm fine. Really."

Joe mumbled an expletive as if he didn't like the choice they had to make for Martin's sake. "OK, but don't try to rush," he ordered. "Take it nice and easy."

Nice and easy, she cautioned herself. As long as she could bend her knee, she was fine. It was better to spend a few extra minutes and deliver Martin downstairs in one piece than hurry and risk her knee giving out completely. As strong as Joe was, he couldn't carry both of them.

Step by agonizing step, she followed, grateful for those brief stops when Joe claimed he needed to catch his breath, even though he wasn't breathing hard. "Almost there," he encouraged.

The faded number one on the stairwell door was the most beautiful sight she'd seen. Although she tried to hide her relief after they slid Martin into the back of the ambulance, she suspected Joe had heard her tired sigh and seen her pronounced limp.

"Can you drive?" he asked. "If not, you can ride in the back."

"I didn't break, Joe," she said waspishly, although a tiny spot inside her was pleased by his concern. "I can still drive, so take care of our patient."

When they arrived at the hospital and gave their report, Martin's condition had remained unchanged.

"I see what you mean," Dr. Mike told them as he examined the spot Maggie had drawn his attention to on Martin's skull. "We'll get a CT scan and see what's going on inside his head."

"Let us know how it turns out," Joe said.

"Will do."

"We also need someone to check out my

partner," he told Dr. Mike. "She banged up her knee and her hip."

"I tripped," she said, "and I fell hard, but I'm able to walk."

"We'd better take a look." He waved a nurse over and before Maggie could say "estimated time of arrival" she was ushered into a treatment room with Joe.

"This is so unnecessary," she complained to both.

"Then we'll be out of here before the ink dries on the paperwork," he said with equanimity. "But we aren't leaving until I know you're OK."

"Oh, for heaven's sake. I've fallen before and—"

"Then, like he said, honey," the middle-aged, no-nonsense nurse said, "you'll be on your way in a few minutes. Meantime, drop your pants."

Maggie's hands went to her belt buckle, then stopped. "Not while he's in the room."

The R.N. glanced at Joe as she thumbed toward the room's exit. "You heard her."

He grinned. "I'm going, but I'll be right outside if you need me."

As soon as he left, she faced Maggie. "Protective, is he?"

"Yeah, and I don't know where that streak came

from." She pushed her trousers down her legs, ignoring the golfball-sized knot and growing bruise on her hip to study her now purplish and slightly swollen knee. "We're just partners."

"Uh-huh." The woman raised a disbelieving eyebrow. "Whatever you say."

"We are," Maggie insisted.

"Sure thing, honey. Just keep telling yourself that, but it won't make it so."

CHAPTER SEVEN

SHORTLY after the nurse escorted a physician's assistant into Maggie's exam cubicle, Joe relaxed against the wall with his arms folded as if he didn't have a care in the world. Inside, however, his thoughts were in turmoil. He didn't like the idea of Maggie getting hurt. And she *was* hurt. Oh, she tried hard not to show it, but he'd heard the crack of bone against the concrete. He'd seen bigger and tougher guys brought to tears for lesser accidents.

It was too easy to blame the three guys who'd gotten physical before he and Maggie had traveled down those stairs. If the one hadn't bounced her across the floor moments earlier, she might have been her usual sure-footed self. Adrenaline had helped him make short work of the two who'd ganged up on him, but he'd still been a split second too late. Even now, thinking of what might have happened was enough to twist his gut into a hard knot.

The only thought keeping him sane was that the three sleazeballs hadn't pulled a knife or a gun. They'd obviously expected that robbing a couple of paramedics, especially as one was a slender female, would be as easy as snatching a purse from a little old lady, but Maggie had surprised them. In fact, she'd surprised *him* and he knew her better than a lot of men knew their wives in the non-biblical sense. He'd seen how hard she worked at her job, how she pushed herself during their training sessions, and how determined she was to be an asset rather than a liability. The worst thing he could ever do was treat her like "a girl". There wasn't room for that attitude in their department.

Yet, it had always been obvious to him that she demanded more of herself because of her gender and today it had paid off. Her entire leg had to have hurt like the devil as they'd carted Kazinsky down those four flights, especially after she'd tripped, but she'd dug in and done it anyway. Without complaining, too.

The door to her exam room opened and both the PA and the nurse stepped out. Immediately, he stood at attention. "How is she?"

"She'll live," the PA, identified as Sybil by her name badge, answered with the lightest twitch to her mouth, as if she found his question amusing.

"Can I go in?"

"Yeah, but give her a few minutes. I doubt if she'd appreciate you charging in on her before she zips her pants."

"Does she need to be relieved of duty?" He was already rehearsing his story for the captain and imagining the paperwork involved.

"I'm leaving the decision to her," Sybil answered. "If she puts ice on her knee and doesn't run any of your running-up-five-flights-of-stairs drills or practice a fireman carry, she should be fine. If she has any problems, though, she needs to come back and see us."

"OK." The two moved away and Joe hesitated outside the door. He wanted to rush in and see for himself that she was as fine as Sybil claimed, but Maggie wouldn't appreciate his concern. *Patience,* he told himself as he knocked.

At her quiet "Come in" he entered to find her buckling her belt. They'd been apart for less than thirty minutes and he felt as if hours had passed. Assured she wasn't writhing in pain and hiding it under a stiff upper lip, his worry lifted.

Now all he had to do was concentrate on something besides the fact they were alone in a cozy cubicle that didn't even have a window.

"Sybil told me you're OK," he said.

She smiled wryly. "Did you have any doubt?"

"To be honest, yes. You hit the concrete hard and that was after those scumbags tossed you across the floor."

She frowned. "Oh, for the love of pete... You're being completely ridiculous and unreasonable. If anyone else had gotten into a tussle with some low-lifes, you both would have bragged about your bruises. And if anyone else had tripped on the stairs, you would have told him to walk it off and quit being a baby."

"Probably," he agreed.

"Then why can't you treat me the same?"

"Because you aren't the same. Because..." He had to kiss her. It was the only way he could reassure himself that she was OK. *Just one kiss.*

"Because what?"

"Because when I'm with you, I want to do this." His objective was simple—to taste her lips and be gone before she could protest. In one swift move he stepped forward, pulled her into his arms, and covered her mouth with his.

His plan blew up faster than kindling doused in gasoline. He hadn't expected her to respond so sweetly. He hadn't expected her hands to drift onto his upper arms then his shoulders, before settling around his neck.

He certainly hadn't expected to have this undeniable urge to rip her clothes off until nothing lay between them. Luckily, enough brain cells were still working for him to restrain himself. Barely.

"You're really OK?" he muttered against her lips.

"I'm fine. Truly."

Slowly, he released her, wishing they could stay here, cocooned in this tiny room, but it wasn't possible. Not only were they on duty but someone would need this space for a patient. More importantly, though, he didn't have anything to offer a woman like Maggie and he couldn't pretend that he did.

"We'd better go," he said, switching his mental gears from concerned admirer to professional partner as he ushered her to the door. "The captain is probably wondering what happened to us."

Apparently she wasn't willing to dissect what had happened any more than he was because she simply nodded. "Can we keep my mishap our secret? I'd rather everyone not know I was so clumsy."

"They'll wonder why you're icing your knee," he pointed out. "And don't think you won't because I'll make sure you do."

"I know, but…" she winced "…I hate to tell the guys I tripped over a mouse. A tiny, loveable, little mouse. I'll never hear the end of their teasing."

"Just think of all the diseases those critters carry."

"I know, but a *mouse.*" She waited. "Why not a pit-bull or a Doberman? Something ferocious?"

He shrugged. "We'll tell them it wasn't tiny." He moved his hands about six inches apart. "It was the biggest mouse either of us had ever seen. And it was so big, it knocked you over with one sweep of its tail." He slowed his step to accommodate her limp.

"I don't think they'll buy your story," she said wryly.

"Maybe not, but we can try." He steered her toward the passenger side of the ambulance, but she balked.

"I can drive."

"I'm sure you can," he said, ignoring her protest. "But humor me."

"You like being in charge, don't you?" she asked lightly.

He started to protest, then stopped. Taking charge, leading and not following, was a legacy of being left to the mercy and kindness of strangers through no fault of his own. Choosing his own destiny had become important to him as a kid. However, that didn't mean he chafed under authority—he'd simply learned to control whatever he could and accept the situations he couldn't.

"Is it obvious?" he asked wryly.

She laughed. "Only to me."

Back at the fire station, after a short visit with the captain and a quick shower to remove the smell clinging to him from their last call, Joe joined Maggie in the common room, where Maggie's fears had obviously come to pass. One by one, each member of the crew was regaling her with mouse jokes.

"You told your tale," he commented as he sank beside her on the sofa where she was icing her knee as ordered. "No pun intended."

"I had to," she mourned.

"No one bought the giant rodent story?"

She smiled. "No, and I told it quite well, too.

including beady red eyes, twitchy whiskers, and teeth as long as my palm."

He laughed at her description. "Too bad. Better luck next time."

"Hey, Maggie," Jimbo called out. "How do you save a drowning mouse?"

He saw her visibly clench her teeth. "I have no idea," she ground out.

"Give him mouse-to-mouse resuscitation."

She groaned as the more boisterous crew members hooted and hollered. "That's bad."

Jimbo snickered from his place in front of the computer. "I thought it was rather clever. Just found it on the Internet."

"Yeah, well, thanks for the chuckles," she said wryly.

Joe had no sooner decided he should rescue Maggie from a night of mouse stories when the opportunity presented itself. "Hey, Joe," Shep called out. "Don't you have any jokes to share in Maggie's honor?"

"Sure," he said, clicking the television remote to change the broadcast to the sports channel, "but I've already been warned to keep them to myself. She's got that look in her eye, so I will."

"What look?" Shep asked.

"You know. The one where I'll be enjoying peanut butter and jelly sandwiches and sugar-free vanilla wafers the next time she cooks instead of chicken primavera and chocolate caramel turtle bars. My stomach's not willing to risk it." He paused for effect. "Is yours?"

"She's got her famous primavera on the menu?" Shep asked eagerly.

Joe had no idea, but he wasn't above stretching the truth. "We talked about it," he said.

"I see your point, Donatelli." Jimbo nodded thoughtfully. "Nothing is worth gambling away chicken primavera. Your partner drives a hard bargain."

Joe laughed. "She does, doesn't she?"

His ploy worked because the mouse references faded away and baseball became the topic of conversation. While everyone was deep in the discussion about which team had the most promising players, Joe glanced at Maggie.

"Thanks," she mouthed.

Her smile of gratitude caused the satisfied feeling in his chest to swell until he didn't have room left for anything else. Funny thing, he'd never seen himself as being a champion of the underdog, defender of the down-trodden. Not that Maggie was down-trodden, but in this situation she was definitely the underdog. And to his surprise, he liked playing the role.

But being Maggie's champion was different than being Breanna's. If he failed Maggie, no harm done. She could handle whatever setbacks came her way. Breanna was different. Oh, one could argue that he shared a unique bond with her—he understood feelings of rejection and abandonment better than most—but the responsibility of caring for a child was enough to give a man nightmares. If he failed her… He didn't want to think about the consequences.

If Maggie hadn't been reflecting on Joe's kiss in the E.R. as she'd returned to the common room after a quick shower to scrub off Tattoo Hands' touch as well as the boarding house's residual smell, she might have been able to hide the evidence of her sore knee. But, no, she'd been too busy replaying those stolen moments to pay attention to what she'd been doing. In fact, they should have discussed their brief lapse of judgment on the way back to the station, but she'd been too grateful to think about something other than her scuffle with the obvious ringleader and what might have been to make an issue of it.

And so she'd favored her leg as she'd gone into the kitchen and Harry had immediately noticed her limp. Word had spread faster than a cold virus and the barrage had begun before she'd made herself an ice pack.

Thanks to Joe's subtle blackmail, the teasing had stopped as abruptly as it had started and her thoughts had quickly returned to those moments of being in Joe's arms.

Looking at the situation logically, getting involved with each other wasn't a good idea. Sure, they could work around the departmental policies, but the timing was all wrong. Would he have been attracted to her or acted on that attraction if he hadn't needed her help with Breanna?

It was also entirely possible that he was simply acting out of gratitude. Her relationship with Arthur had begun somewhat similarly and she'd read more into their first kiss than she should have.

Although she had to admit that Joe's kisses were beyond compare. His passion, his hunger, his barely held restraint was very different from Arthur's gentleness and near-hesitation. Joe took the concept of pleasant to a whole new level—one where a toe-curling ache drove good sense right out of her head.

But if what had happened in that E.R. cubicle hadn't been enough to surprise her, his defense in the middle of the crew's harmlessly persistent teasing was. A few short weeks ago he probably would have chimed in, too, but his obvious consideration for her feelings was a clear sign they were becoming an efficient team instead of two individuals who merely worked together.

Because she found hope in their situation, she was certain there was hope for Breanna's, too. He needed his little girl to soften his rough edges every bit as much as his daughter needed him, regardless of what his precious DNA test showed.

If she was being honest with herself, she'd admit that she wanted Joe to need her, too, because she wanted to teach him what love really meant, to convince him that loving someone was a positive, fulfilling experience.

Unfortunately, for every two steps forward throughout the days that followed, it seemed as if they fell one step behind.

"You can't be serious about this," Maggie protested a week later. They were on their way to pack Dee's personal effects so that everything would be ready for tomorrow, when the guys from the station would provide the muscle to move out her things. Dee's lease would end in ten days and the landlord wanted the furnished apartment vacated, so the task Joe had been postponing couldn't be postponed any longer. However, the chore of packing didn't bother her—what he intended while they were in the neighborhood did.

"Why wouldn't I be serious?" he asked.

"Why hunt for a man who her closest friend and neighbor only saw a handful of times?"

"He obviously met Dee after I left. If he can shed some light on what was going on in her life, why she did what she did, then it won't be a wasted effort," he told her. "If you don't want to help, I'll look for him alone."

"I'll help," she said reluctantly, "but I'm going on record that I think it's a mistake. As Dee's closest friend, Hannah would have known if this guy had been important to her."

"Maybe. Maybe not. All I want to do is talk to him."

Maggie guessed his motives ran deeper than

that, but his squared jaw indicated that he was determined to follow the course he'd set. "I can't convince you to change your mind, can I?"

He shook his head. "No, so don't waste your breath."

"Did anyone ever tell you how single-minded you are?"

"Goal-oriented," he corrected her. "And, yes, I've heard that before."

And so, resigned to that particular task on their to-do list, Maggie helped Joe sort through Dee's possessions. They created three piles—one for keepsakes, one for donations to the local thrift store and crisis center, and one for items destined for the dumpster.

Sorting and packing turned out to be easy. Choosing what Breanna would treasure as she grew older was simply a matter of using her own mother's keepsakes as a guide. The few pieces of jewelry, a few trinkets and figurines, the obviously hand-made sofa throws were a few of the items she carefully boxed for storage while the rest was segregated for their respective destinations.

However, what *was* difficult was watching Breanna crawling from room to room, looking puzzled and occasionally calling "Mama?" as if she expected her mother to appear at any moment.

Eventually, Breanna crawled onto Dee's bed, clutched a handful of the green silk ladies' pajamas lying neatly against the pillows, popped a thumb into her mouth and fell asleep on the patchwork quilt.

The sight broke Maggie's heart again. "Whatever you do," she warned Joe, "keep that nightgown and quilt for her."

Gazing at the little girl curled protectively around the fabric, his eyes grew suspiciously vacant and his voice sounded hollow, as if he, too, recognized its importance. "I will," he promised.

Later, while Hannah watched over Breanna, Maggie accompanied Joe to the various apartments in Dee's building, as well as the restaurant where she'd worked.

Only one person remembered seeing her with the fellow Hannah had described but, like Dee's neighbor, she didn't know his name or what he'd had in common with Dee.

As Joe drove away from the Prairie Pines Apartment complex, he seemed overly quiet.

"Are you disappointed we didn't dig up any leads?" she asked.

"Yes." He paused. "And no. Yes, because I can't help wondering if he's in a better position to take care of Breanna than I am."

"If he was, don't you think Dee would have made him Breanna's legal guardian?" she said practically. "Give her some credit, will you?"

"You're right. I have to trust she knew what she was doing and had method in her madness."

"Exactly. Besides, this guy could have been anyone from an insurance salesman to a bill collector."

He turned a sheepish face to her. "I never thought of that."

"You should," she declared. "So tell me about the half of you that's *not* disappointed we hit a dead end."

He exhaled a long sigh as he glanced at the child between them. "The little one is starting to grow on me."

She understood precisely what he was talking about, but Breanna wasn't the only person who'd grown on her. Breanna's father had, too.

"That's the way it works, Joe," she said quietly. "The more time you spend with an individual, the easier it is to love them."

A thoughtful expression crossed his face, but

he didn't say a word and Maggie didn't belabor the point. She might recognize how maintaining emotional distance was his way to protect himself from loving and losing the people who'd become important to him, but he had to experience his own epiphany.

Idly, Maggie wondered if Dee had tried to teach Joe that concept but in the end had been forced to settle for friendship. Could it be that Fate was giving her the opportunity to continue the lesson? And if she took up the challenge, would she be more successful than Dee had been or would she, too, have to settle for crumbs?

As risky as the idea was, as high as the odds were against her, she wanted to try. She wanted to mean more and be more than his safety net. She wanted to prove to him that caring for someone didn't have to be painful, that loving someone would finally fill those empty spaces inside him.

She wanted to make him whole because then he just might be willing to consider how good the two of them were together.

After Joe had put Breanna to bed, he settled in front of the television to watch a rerun of an old favorite on TV. But instead of paying attention to the plot, he pondered Maggie's comment in the context of his own relationships. He'd never dated the same woman more than a few times because none had ever held his interest for longer than that. If Dee hadn't become more friend than lover, she would have fallen into that category, too.

The only real exception to his unconscious habit was Maggie. He couldn't explain it, but she made him feel as if he could do everything and fail at nothing. She made him wonder what it would be like to create a family with someone who loved him. A month ago he would have labeled the idea impossible and instantly dismissed it, but not now. Now she made him *wish* for the impossible.

But as an hour drifted past and Breanna woke up cranky and inconsolable, Joe changed his wish to something more within reach…like getting her to go back to sleep.

Unfortunately, nothing he tried worked. At 11:00 p.m. he speed-dialed Maggie on his cellphone. "I need you," he said without preamble.

"Wh-what?"

From the tone of her voice she'd obviously been asleep. He might have felt guilty, but desperation overruled.

"I'm sorry to wake you, but it's Breanna."

Instantly, she sounded alert. "What's wrong?"

"She won't quit crying."

"Did you change her? Feed her?"

He fought the urge to snap. Yelling at Maggie wouldn't solve his problems. "I did all those things," he said as patiently as possible, holding an unhappy baby in one arm. "I've walked her, sung until I'm hoarse, but nothing I do makes a difference."

"What about her temperature? Does she seem sick?"

"She's warm, but I think it's because she's been crying for so long. Please, Maggie, I'm begging you. Can you come?"

"I'll be right over."

Relieved that help was on the way, he bounced Breanna against his shoulder. "Did you hear that?" he crooned as he paced the floor. "Maggie's coming. You should feel better now." He certainly did.

Unfortunately, Breanna didn't appear impressed or consoled with his news. She simply rubbed her eyes, screwed up her mouth and, with her lower lip trembling, let loose another wail.

"Maggie will fix whatever's wrong," he murmured. "You'll see."

For the next fifteen minutes he walked a circle through his house, starting with his living room, down the hall to the bedrooms, back around to the kitchen, before finally returning to the living room. When the doorbell rang, he'd never heard a nicer sound.

"She won't stop crying," he told Maggie as she discarded her lightweight windbreaker over a chair.

"Maybe she's teething."

Why hadn't he considered that? He should have. Some father he was, he thought in disgust. He moved his hand to her mouth, then reconsidered. "She'll bite."

"If that's the problem, rubbing will soothe the pain."

Joe watched her run an index finger along Breanna's gum line as the little girl squirmed in his arms. "I can't feel anything," she said before she peered into her mouth, "and her gums don't look red or swollen. Have you noticed her pulling at her ears like they hurt?"

He shook his head. "No, but before I take her to the emergency room, let's see if she'll be happier with you."

As he held the little girl toward Maggie, the

baby dove into her arms with enthusiasm. While she snuffled softly against Maggie's neck, the tension in Joe's shoulders eased. "I should have phoned you sooner," he said wryly.

"We'll see how long this lull lasts."

To Joe's disappointment, Breanna soon tired of Maggie and the scene repeated itself.

"I'd been hoping we wouldn't go through this again." He rubbed at the ridge between his eyebrows. "It's been nearly a week since we had a night like this. I hate feeling so helpless."

"Well, we have to do something," Maggie declared. "Let's try a warm bath and a fresh nightgown."

Grateful to be doing something, *anything,* Joe did as instructed, but in the end, as he held her on his lap with her bunny, Breanna still wouldn't be appeased. She fussed and wiggled until he felt as if holding her was like trying to hold a restless tiger cub.

Maggie's eyes suddenly gleamed with an idea. "Joe," she began, "where's the quilt and silk nightie we brought back with us today?"

"Still in the box in the garage with the rest of the things I'm keeping." As he recalled Breanna's attachment to the fabric earlier today, he caught on to Maggie's idea. "Do you think that's what she wants?"

"It's worth a try. I'll be right back."

As soon as she returned and handed the silky garment to Breanna, the change was instantaneous. The little girl sat up, reached out and clutched the material against her before she settled against Joe's chest, one fist buried in the silk and the other hand clutching her bunny. "Mama," she mumbled as she closed her eyes and became boneless in Joe's lap.

Joe glanced at Maggie, hardly able to believe the sudden transformation. "I can't believe it," he whispered.

"Neither can I. I wish I'd thought of it sooner, the poor baby. It's probably the one thing that reminds her of her mother."

Joe scooted to the edge of the sofa and rose. "I'll try putting her to bed."

"Good idea."

Maggie followed him into Breanna's room and watched him tenderly lay the youngster in her crib, tuck the silk gown against her, then cover her with her comforter. With a soft touch that seemed incongruous with his large hands, he smoothed her hair away from her small face, then moved toward the door. "Are you coming?" he whispered.

"In a minute. I want to make sure she doesn't wake up."

"OK."

Alone, Maggie brushed a kiss on the little girl's forehead, wishing she could magically take away all the pain and hurt and frustration the youngster felt. It was possible, she decided, but the only magical thing that would work was the love and security she and Joe could provide.

"Sweet dreams," she murmured, then slipped out and left the door slightly ajar. Searching for Joe, she found him in the kitchen, standing in front of the refrigerator, removing a bottle of beer.

"Whoever coined the words 'Silence is golden' knew what they were talking about," she said fervently.

"I'll say." He raised the brown bottle into the air. "Want one?"

"Please."

He handed it to her, then got his own.

"You've had quite a night," she remarked.

"No kidding."

His tone was clipped, his expression halfway between grim and impassive. "Joe?" she asked.

carefully. "You do realize you should be happy she's asleep."

"I am." He took a long swig from his bottle.

"You don't seem too happy to me."

He headed into the living room and dropped onto the sofa. "Why wouldn't I be?"

"I don't know. You just seem…upset."

"I'm fine. Just go home, Maggie." He sounded weary as he leaned back against the cushion and closed his eyes, loosely cradling his drink in his hands.

Something was wrong. She'd expected him to beg her to stay, like he had the first night Breanna had been so distraught. Now he was practically booting her out the door.

"I will, after I know why you're acting so strangely."

He opened his eyes and met her gaze. "Strange? What makes you say that?"

She shook her head. "Deny it all you want, but I know you well enough to know you have something on your mind."

He took another swallow as if to bide his time, but Maggie refused to budge. "I'll sit here all night if I have to," she threatened.

For several long, painful seconds she waited,

until finally he spoke. "It's my fault she had a rough evening."

"Your fault?" she echoed. "How?"

"I never should have taken her with us today," he said. "I should have known seeing her home would bring back memories, open up old wounds of missing her mother, but I didn't stop to consider how it might affect her. Instead, I was selfish and wanted her with me."

"You weren't selfish." She moved to sit on the coffee table in front of him. "I can understand why you'd hesitate to leave her with a sitter again, even one as great as Nancy. As for not thinking about how she'd be affected by going back to a familiar place, I'm guilty, too."

He didn't seem convinced. "Maybe, but you figured out what would calm her. I didn't."

"It was a lucky guess."

He shook his head. "It was more than luck."

"Don't be ridiculous. You would have eventually gotten the idea."

"When? Her fifth birthday?"

"Sarcasm doesn't become you, Joe. OK, so I thought of something to try. You would have, too, if you hadn't been so exhausted. I was fresher and less frustrated than you were. That's all."

He finished his beer, his gaze distant and speculative, as if he was on the verge of making a decision. A life-changing decision for all of them. A decision that probably wouldn't bode well for anyone, including Joe.

Maggie narrowed her gaze. "Don't you dare tell me you're giving up," she warned.

"It would be for the best," he began.

"What? Best for who?" She paused. "If you do this, I'll…"

He studied her with curiosity. "You'll what?"

What could she say? She'd never speak to him again? As threats went, it was weak, but if he had to be threatened to keep Breanna, did she want him to?

On the other hand, maybe he simply needed someone to shut down his pity party…

"You're right," she said coolly. "Go ahead and break your promise to me and to Dee. Wave your white flag of surrender. You've wanted an escape clause since the first day you got her. Far be it from me to convince you to do the right thing."

She rose and leaned over him. "You're so quick to tell me how you're afraid of being like your father who ran when the going got tough.

Maybe you two *are* more alike than you thought or I imagined."

Warming to her subject, she added, "In fact, I don't think you should wait until morning. Do it now. While she's asleep. She can wake up in her new home." She stormed into the garage for an empty box, then returned to find him standing in the middle of his living room.

She shoved the cardboard container in his arms so hard he stumbled backward. "Here. I made it easy for you to start packing. Better yet, I'll help you."

She yanked the box away from him and knelt in front of Breanna's toy basket. Immediately, she began tossing in the rings, the stacking blocks, and then her stuffed lion and giraffe, waiting, *expecting* Joe to stop her.

He didn't.

By the time she got to the bedtime story books, her hands were shaking with suppressed fury, but her anger quickly turned to pain as she stroked the colorful covers and remembered how Breanna had snuggled against her as she'd read the stories. As she realized she might not read those books to little Bee again, tears filled her eyes.

Yet it was more than the potential loss of

Breanna that made her heart ache. It was knowing she would lose Joe, too, because the two were a package deal. A few hours earlier she'd decided to convince him that loving someone didn't have to be painful. How ironic to be proving how painful it could be.

Suddenly, a large hand covered hers. "What are you doing?" he asked in her ear.

She cleared her throat and rubbed away the wetness on her face. "I'm packing."

"Don't."

"Why not?" She waited until she'd regained her composure before twisting herself around to study his face, the same handsome face that was lined with weariness and shadowed with determination.

"Because Breanna needs her toys," he said simply. "She isn't going anywhere."

"Are you sure, Joe? Really *sure?*"

"Of course I am. My thirty days aren't over yet." He paused. "Are you OK now?"

As she held the books in her white-knuckled grip, she searched for the right words. "I was re-membering the first time I read these books to her. The thought of never doing it again got to me."

"I know."

"Do you know something else?" she asked.

"I'm jealous. Horribly, bitterly, jealous because you've been gifted with this precious child and don't know what to do with her, while I would give *anything* to be in your shoes. I'm like the bridesmaid who's never a bride, the aunt who's never a mother. It was hard enough to live through the first time, but believe me when I say the second is much, much worse. And..." Her voice faded for an instant.

"And..." she cleared her throat "...I don't know if I can go through it again."

Upset at herself for revealing her most private thoughts, she rose, but before she could put distance between them, Joe was pulling her close. She held herself stiffly, refusing to accept the comfort he offered.

"I'd never realized..." he said hoarsely.

"Now you do."

"As glad as I am to hear what's going through your pretty head, your basic premise was wrong."

She raised her chin to meet his gaze. "Oh?"

"I wasn't giving up."

Her eyes narrowed and this time, when she tried to leave his embrace, he let her. "I saw the look on your face."

"I'll admit I was disappointed and frustrated."

"But why? Everything turned out—"

He cut her off. "Because *I* wanted to be the one who knew what to do. *I* wanted to be the one with the answers, the one who rode in to save the day."

Now she really was confused. "But if you wanted those things, why did you call me?"

"Because I couldn't deliver," he said simply. "Oh, I could have waited her out, I suppose, but that route seemed cruel. I phoned you because I couldn't put my wants above her needs."

Remorse struck her in the solar plexus as she realized how badly she'd misjudged him. "Oh, Joe."

"As for giving up, we had this conversation before. I told you then that I wouldn't do anything without talking to you first. Did you forget, or could it be that you still don't trust me?"

As much as it pained her to admit the truth, she had to be honest. He'd see anything else as the excuse it was.

"Some of both," she admitted. "You looked so unhappy and yet so determined…I'm sorry."

Anticipating him hurt by her obvious lack of faith, she was surprised when she saw calm acceptance in his expression, as if he appreciated her candor.

"Under those circumstances, I can't blame you," he admitted. "The fact is, I *had* come to a decision. I can't continue like this either." He ignored her gasp. "I want you to move in with us."

CHAPTER EIGHT

MAGGIE'S jaw dropped. "Excuse me?"

"Move in with us," Joe repeated, undaunted by her shock. "I know this comes as a surprise. I was surprised myself when the idea hit me, but it makes perfect sense."

A wrinkle appeared on her brow and her eyes narrowed slightly. "How?"

"The next time we have a crisis, the next time *Breanna* has a crisis," he corrected himself, "you'll be here."

"I'm only a few minutes away," she pointed out. "Crying doesn't constitute an emergency. And if there *was* an emergency, may I remind you that you're trained to handle one as easily as I."

"Breanna needs a woman in her life."

"She has Nancy."

"Only one day out of three. It isn't enough."

"I'm already here for most of the other two. And when I'm not, she's asleep."

Joe pulled out what he thought was his strongest argument. "You love her and she loves you."

"There is that," she said with equanimity. "But what about our jobs? This won't go down well with the powers that be."

"The captain knows you're helping me."

"Helping isn't the same as living together. Besides, think of how difficult it will be when we're working. We'll have to weigh our every word and action so no one will suspect. But even then, someone is bound to figure out what we're doing and then we'll have to pay the piper."

She had a point, but he refused to back down easily. "If you won't move in, I'll hire Nancy to live here 24/7."

"You'd resort to blackmail?"

He nodded. "Yes."

"I see." Then, "Why do you want this so badly?"

Joe expected to see some indecision on her face, as if she were weighing her options, but he only saw curiosity and it puzzled him.

"I've just spent the last five minutes telling you."

"Then it's all about Breanna."

"Of course." But as soon as he spoke, he knew

he wasn't being completely honest. He wanted her there for him, too. She gave him a hope and a confidence that no one else had.

"Are you asking in terms of permanent or temporary?" she asked.

Her question didn't surprise him. Maggie believed in commitment even if he did not, although inviting her to move in was as close as he could come to giving her the permanence she wanted and deserved.

Still, the lure of an enduring arrangement was strong enough to be disturbing to his long-held belief system. "Nothing lasts for ever," he reminded her.

She hesitated, a small frown marring her expression. "Do you ever think about the future? Not just next week or next month, but the future in terms of five or ten years from now?"

"Of course I do," he said, mildly affronted. "I wouldn't have gotten where I am today if I hadn't planned ahead and worked toward my goals."

"I was talking about your *personal* future, not your professional one."

He'd learned never to include another person in his long-range plans because he didn't trust anyone to be reliable enough to remain there.

However, now that she'd drawn his attention to his habit, his future did seem rather lonely. Lonely or not, though, he'd also learned not to look for or borrow trouble. It came on its own, without any help.

"Isn't there a bit of folk wisdom that says if one worries about today, tomorrow will take care of itself? If you follow that philosophy, today Breanna needs a mother."

"She probably does," Maggie agreed.

His spirits rose. "Then you'll—"

"No."

He stared at her, unable to believe she'd turned down what she wanted most—the very thing he was offering her. "No?"

"No," she said firmly. "If all I wanted was to be Breanna's mother, I'd be tempted to accept. To me, though, it isn't enough.

"I also know that 'for ever' isn't in your vocabulary," she continued, "and you avoid ties like they were an infectious disease. You probably also think your upbringing somehow puts you at a disadvantage and makes you less worthy than you are."

She'd metaphorically read his mail! Her accurate assessment had his jaw dropping in surprise.